RUSTLER'S RANGE

Tad Strong's bold attempt to capture the outlaw king in his own domain, and make his escape, had gone badly wrong. In retreat, he was propped against the wall; pinned down, surrounded, and hopelessly outnumbered. Overwhelmed by the constant barrage of bullets and splintering wood — he was doomed. At least he would die thinking of Becky . . . He'd failed to complete his mission. Now, all he could do was to wait for the final bullet . . .

BILLY HALL

RUSTLER'S RANGE

Complete and Unabridged

LINFORD
Leicester

First published in Great Britain in 2009 by
Robert Hale Limited
London

First Linford Edition
published 2010
by arrangement with
Robert Hale Limited
London

British Library CIP Data

Hall, Billy.
  Rustler's range. - -
  (Linford western library)
  1. Western stories.
  2. Large type books.
  I. Title II. Series
  823.9'14–dc22

  ISBN 978–1–44480–436–2

Published by
F. A. Thorpe (Publishing)
Anstey, Leicestershire

Set by Words & Graphics Ltd.
Anstey, Leicestershire
Printed and bound in Great Britain by
T. J. International Ltd., Padstow, Cornwall

This book is printed on acid-free paper

1

Sudden hush, like a tidal wave, swept along the dusty main street. It swallowed all noise in its rush. Its enveloping grip of sudden silence turned heads two blocks down the street. Eyes darted here and there, seeking the source of the sudden, eerie quiet. It was as if the whole town itself suddenly held its breath.

The source was not hard to find. Tad Strong stood stock still in the center of the dirt street. His six-foot-one frame looked almost relaxed. Almost. Except for the hand resting just against the butt of the big Russian .44 on his hip.

It was a big handgun. Too big for gunfighters, generally. Its size and weight made it just a blink too slow for the speed of draw that often meant the difference between life and death. The fact that its cylinder held nine rounds, compared to the Colt's six, was of little value if it didn't also have the first shot.

For Tad, the difference didn't seem to matter. His uncanny strength and speed more than offset the weapon's extra size and weight.

His flinty blue eyes watched unblinkingly in the bright Wyoming sun. Almost relaxed. His stance evoked the same sense of 'relaxed' one notices watching a rattlesnake coiled to strike.

Fifty feet away from him, standing slightly spraddle-legged, a young man, scarcely beyond his teens, stared back. His stance was more rigid, tense, expectant. The hand hovering close to the grip of a short-barreled .40-caliber Colt six-shooter flexed constantly. It would open wide, with the fingers splayed far apart, then close to a fist before repeating the maneuver. He leaned slightly forward, balanced on the balls of feet clad in highly polished boots. His pants and shirt, as well as the hat pulled low over his eyes, were same coal black. Even the gunbelt and holster were black leather. They, too, bore unmistakable signs of either bootblack or a lot of saddle soap and polishing. The trace of a smile toyed at the corners of his mouth.

Tad's quiet voice broke the uncanny silence. 'You got no need to do this, kid. I got no quarrel with you.'

The traces of that smile vanished from the younger man's visage. He almost snarled in answer, 'Don't call me 'kid'! The name's Trace Bane.'

'That the name your Ma gave you, or did you make it up?'

The younger man's face tinged red instantly. His eyes flashed. 'I got it from killin' a lot o' better men than you,' he snarled.

'You don't need to prove nothin' here, son,' Tad urged again. 'Just turn over your gun while you're in town, and go have a drink. Enjoy yourself while you're in town.'

'I don't give my gun to no man,' the kid retorted.

'Then you'll have to leave town. We

got an ordinance against packin' a gun in town.'

'Then take it from me,' the young gunman challenged.

'I'd rather not do that. You got too much life to live yet to toss it away now.'

'The only way I'd toss it away is if you could beat me to the draw. There ain't been nobody fast enough to do that yet.'

'There's always somebody faster than you,' Tad responded. 'If not me, somebody else will come along. If you keep pushin', you'll end up pushin' up grass from the bottom side, sooner or later.'

'Then it'll be later,' the youngster snapped.

As he spoke, his hand grabbed the short-barreled Colt. Its light weight and short barrel made it the perfect design for unbeatable speed. It lifted from the holster too swiftly for the eye to follow its upward arc. It leveled, aimed at the badge on the chest of the big man.

The roar of a shell's explosion was a split instant too quick, much too loud for the small-caliber Colt. Even before the sound reached the ears of the breathless audience on the board sidewalks, a driving force slammed into the chest of the young gunman. It drove the breath from him, knocking him backward a step, preventing his finger from squeezing the trigger of his Colt.

He grunted in pain and surprise. He frowned in confusion. He looked at the lawman, seeing, as if in slow motion, the tendril of smoke drifting upward from the Russian .44's barrel.

He looked at his own gun, wondering for just an instant, why it was tumbling from his hand.

His confusion faded into a momentary dizziness, then oblivion. He was dead before his carefully clad body was soiled by the dust of the street.

Tad watched him for a long moment, assuring himself the youngster was no further threat. He emitted a long sigh as he holstered the big pistol.

As if the act released some unseen restraint, sudden chatter erupted all along the street.

'That fella was fast!'

'Plumb greased lightnin', all right.'

'Did you see the marshal draw?'

'Nope. I saw the kid grab 'is gun. Then I looked at the marshal, and his gun was already out, fired, and smoke a-driftin' up from the barrel.'

'How'd he haul it out that quick?'

'Same as always. I seen him do it three times now. I ain't sure he's totally human. There ain't no way a human man can be that fast.'

The lone feminine voice yet heard spoke up. 'I think it's absolutely barbaric to see disagreements have to be settled by somebody getting killed. It's uncivilized. There is no justification for that kind of violence.'

Her strident assertions momentarily restored the silence on the street. Then a faceless voice said, 'Preach that sermon to the kid. Maybe he'll change his mind about forcin' the marshal to draw.'

Several men laughed, causing the protesting woman to turn and huff her way off down the street.

'Are you Tad Strong?'

The one with the badge eyed the middle-aged man facing him on the board sidewalk. The worn clothing and weathered visage marked him as one who had spent his life outdoors. Thick, calloused, scarred hands, looked strong enough to crush a rock to gravel. The clear, almost green eyes that stared back at the marshal signaled an open honesty typical of the breed who had settled the wild country. He nodded wordlessly.

The stranger thrust out a hand. 'My name's Ezra Bingham. Most folks call me Grunt.'

Tad took the offered hand, returning its firm grip. He almost smiled. If it hadn't been so soon after being forced to end a young life so senselessly, he probably would have. 'Grunt?'

Bingham nodded, offering a small, almost rueful grin of his own. 'I sorta tend to grunt whenever I'm strainin' to do anything. Just a habit I picked up somewhere. Folks sorta like to make fun of it.'

'Well, I guess gruntin's better'n whinin',' Tad observed. 'What can I do for you?'

'Go to work for me,' Bingham said instantly.

Tad's eyebrows shot up. 'Well now, that's short and to the point.'

'I don't spend a lot o' time with small talk,' Bingham explained.

'I sorta noticed that.'

'If you're interested, I'd be proud to buy you a cup o' coffee an' tell you what I got in mind.'

'Is it somethin' I might be interested in?'

Ezra shrugged. 'I hope so. I'll make it worth your while.'

'Honest work?'

'I wouldn't never ask a man to do nothin' else.'

'Well, then, let's have that cup of coffee. I'll listen, at least.'

Rather than to an eating place, Tad led the way to the town marshal's office. Inside, a large coffee pot sat on the back of the pot-bellied stove. Its presence explained the heat given off by the stove, even though the day was more than sufficiently warm without it.

'Me and Cliff sorta got a habit o' havin' the coffee pot on all the time,' Tad explained.

'Cliff?'

'He's the town marshal. I'm just the deputy.'

'Gets a mite strong by the end o' the day doesn't it?' Ezra jutted his chin toward the large, well-blackened coffee pot.

Tad smiled. 'When it gets too thick to run inta the cup, we scrape it out with a flat stick and start over.'

With his first sip, Bingham thought it was getting pretty close to that time. He started to make an appropriate comment, but Tad spoke first. 'So what's on your mind? Who are you? Where you from? What kind of job you lookin' for hands for?'

Against his better judgment, Ezra took a second sip of the hot coffee. That convinced him that talking was probably the better alternative. 'Well, like I told you, my name's Ezra Bingham. Most folks — '

' — call you Grunt,' Tad chimed in and said it together with him.

Bingham didn't seem to notice, or wasn't put off by the unexpected teasing. He continued as if uninterrupted. 'I own the Flyin' E Bar ranch, up above Caldwell City, north-west of Churchville, toward the Snowy Range. We run a couple thousand head o' mostly cross-bred stuff. We're havin' a real problem with rustlers. Rustlers an' more, to tell the truth. Stages get robbed reg'lar. Stories drift in of folks gettin' robbed on the road now an' then. We figger we know who they are, but we ain't got no proof. A couple of the ranchers have hired a gunman or two to find out, and sorta fight back a

10

mite. Tryin' to get some evidence of some kind. They either ended up bushwhacked or run outa the country.'

'Sounds like a bad situation.'

'Real bad,' Bingham agreed. 'Gettin' worse all the time. I've heard of you, from time to time. We're at a point where we just gotta hire somebody that's man enough to stay alive long enough to get the goods on whoever's stealin' us blind. I ain't gonna lie to you, and say it'll be easy. Odds ain't none too good. But if you're willin' to go to work for me, I'll pay you two fifty a month and found, furnish you whatever you need in horses or weapons and ammunition, and have at least a dozen men ready to back your play whenever you need it.'

Tad whistled softly at the unheard of wage offer. 'Who've you hired that didn't work out?'

Bingham sighed thoughtfully before answering. 'Well, Art Blankenship hired a fella named Curly Bill.'

Tad snorted. 'Bill'd take more wages

from the rustlers than he would from you, and work both sides of the fence.'

Bingham nodded knowingly. 'You know him, I see. You're right. That's exactly what we figured out, after a while. Then Had Williamson went clear to Kansas and hired a trouble-shooter named Lance Tuckett.'

'I've heard of him. Never met him. Good reputation, though.'

'Didn't do him any good. He thought he was about onto something, then somebody shot him outa the saddle from a grove o' trees. We found him a day later, already bloated up some.'

'Must've been getting close to some-thing.'

Bingham shrugged. 'Then we put enough pressure on the Territorial Governor and the US Marshal's office they sent out a couple of guys that were supposed to be the cat's meow. One of 'em got himself shot an' the other one left the country soundin' just like a cat meowin', all right enough. After that the Marshal's office said they didn't have anyone that could help us right now, but they'd look into it. By the time they get around to lookin', all there's gonna be left to look into is empty range with all the stock run off.'

'Fella named Forestall ranch up in that country?' Tad asked abruptly.

Bingham's eyebrows shot up. 'Why, yeah. He's my neighbor, next south. You know Bud?'

Tad nodded. 'Knew him some time ago. Rode for him with a trail herd one year.'

'Well whatd'ya know! It's a small world.'

'What happens when the job's done?'

Bingham stared at him with a completely blank expression for several heartbeats. It was immediately evident the rancher hadn't even thought it through that far. He sputtered, 'Well, uh, by Jing I, uh, well, I guess we hadn't thunk it through that far. But there'd sure be at least a foreman's job for you on most any one o' the ranches, or a lawman's job in Churchville. We'd dang sure take care of you, if you'd be wantin' to stay around in them parts.'

Tad stared out the dirty window of the marshal's office almost as if he hadn't been listening. After a long pause he said, 'I've been here too long. Startin' to get stupid young gunslingers just like that kid out there, driftin' in just to have a go at me. They think they'll really be somebody if they can manage to outdraw me. He's the fourth guy I've had to kill this month, that I had no reason to quarrel with at all. They just show up outa nowhere, dead set on forcin' me into a shootout. It makes no sense at all.'

'Reputations do get around in this country,' Bingham agreed.

'When do I start?' Tad asked, proving to be every bit as abrupt as the rancher.

Bingham's thoughtful frown was erased by an ear-to-ear grin. 'You mean you'll do it? Well, by Jing! Start right now, as far's I'm concerned,' he exulted.

There were a certain amount of

things that needed wrapped up. The city marshal needed to be informed he was losing his deputy. Tad had to collect his belongings, pack them into saddle-bags and roll the rest into his bedroll. It didn't take a great deal of time. He had always traveled light.

In spite of his relief to be leaving Cheyenne, Tad felt an almost suffocating sense of foreboding as they rode out together the following morning.

2

Tad rode into Caldwell City slowly. He and Bingham had parted company the day before, well before reaching the town nearest to Bingham's ranch. He knew how to get to the Flying E Bar. He just didn't want to advertise to prying eyes that he was a hired gun, brought in to put a stop to the rampant rustling. The longer it took for that information to get around, the longer his life span had a chance of being. If he was lucky, he just might be able to ride back out again. Luckier than those that preceded him, he reminded himself.

Caldwell City, in spite of its ambitious name, was anything but a city. Its single business street, well rutted, its dirt thoroughly mingled with the inevitable ground-in 'road apples' from countless horses, was much the same as innumerable cow towns along the fringes of civilization.

Caldwell City had two distinctions from the norm, however. It had a well-built two-room schoolhouse, constructed of cut lumber, sporting ample coats of bright red paint. The window frames were as carefully painted in brilliant white, making the building stand out startlingly against the unpainted exteriors of the rest of the main street.

The other distinction was that it boasted not one, but two churches. Each was obviously engaged in an ongoing competition with the other for which was the best kept, most well-painted, and most carefully kept yard. One of the churches flaunted an evidently added-on bell tower, with a massive bell that could be tolled from within the vestibule. The other, having a building that would not accommodate such an appendage, refused to be outdone. It had added a short bell tower attached to the side of the building, with an even larger bell, that could be rung from a rope that ran horizontally through the church wall.

'Hope nobody in town wants to sleep in on Sunday mornin',' Tad thought, as he grinned at the overtly ostentatious efforts at superiority.

Beyond that, three saloons, a general store, a blacksmith, a livery barn, a mercantile & millenary shop, a gunsmith, a saddlery and boot shop, one hotel and one café made up the business district of the would-be city.

For no particular reason he swivelled his head, glancing back at the school house he had already ridden past. As he did, he caught a glimpse of motion that drew his attention sharply.

It was only a barest of glimpses. Even so, he was too well conditioned to trust his reflexes to ignore that flash of movement. 'Someone's in trouble,' he muttered.

He wheeled his horse, nudging the big chestnut gelding to a trot back in that direction. He left the road, angling across empty ground where he could get a better view of the hidden side of the schoolhouse.

He was nearly back to the building when he espied the pair. A passably attractive young woman caught his eye first. She was a little too broad-hipped for her size, but was otherwise well proportioned. Her face was small and flawlessly perfect. Her small, slightly upturned nose was punctuated with a small smattering of light freckles across its bridge. She was backed against the wall of the school, well out of sight of any passers-by. A boyish looking cowboy had her pinned into a corner, from where she had no way of escape. Her eyes were wide with a combination of fright and anger.

Tad slid from the saddle, walking swiftly toward the pair. Neither noticed his approach.

'You're just way too pretty not to kiss,' the cowboy proclaimed. The glee in his voice's tone left no doubt he was immensely enjoying the situation, and had no intention of allowing her to escape his control.

'I wouldn't kiss you for a hundred dollars!' the woman retorted. 'Now move out of my way and leave me alone.'

'Aw, I couldn't do that. I just couldn't let you go walkin' away without even givin' me a kiss. Tell you what. Give me one kiss. Just one. Then I'll let you go.'

'I'd guess you'll be lettin' her go right now,' Tad disagreed.

Both of them jumped as if jabbed by a sharp stick at the unexpected sound of his voice. The cowboy wheeled to face him, his body still effectively blocking any attempt of the woman to escape. His broad shoulders, thick chest, and well-muscled arms belied the initial impression of boyishness. So did the .45 tied low on his right hip.

His face contorted with instant anger at the unwanted interference. 'Nobody invited you to this party,' he snarled.

Tad offered his most disarming grin. 'Really? I would've sworn I heard an invitation.'

'Well you was wrong. Now butt out and leave us alone.'

The grin didn't leave Tad's face, but his eyes were far from smiling. 'I don't think the lady would agree with that idea. I distinctly heard her ask you to move out of her way and leave her alone.'

'That ain't none of your business.'

Tad's expression turned abruptly serious, but carefully non-threatening. As if explaining a complex problem, he said, 'You see now, that's where you're just plumb wrong. Any time I see a two-bit cowpoke trying to force himself on a lady, I figure it's supposed to be my business. Now move out of her way.'

The cowboy's demeanor changed in concert with Tad's. His eyes narrowed. His lips thinned. He stepped half a step to his right, away from the woman. His hand dropped to brush the butt of his .45. His voice went soft, almost husky with intensity. 'Do you think you can make me do that?'

Tad's voice was steady and calm, still

carefully as light as if discussing the weather. 'There's no doubt about it. I can kill you before you get that gun half way out of the holster. If you don't believe me, you can have your try. If you're smart, you'll walk away. If you're not, you'll be carried away.'

The young man's conflicting thoughts were clearly readable on his open face. Anger boiled in him at the interruption of his fun. Confidence in his ability with a gun prodded him to action against this interloper. At the same time, something shouted to his subconscious that this was not a man to challenge. There was something in his easy assurance that he would win a contest of weapons that was neither bluff nor bluster.

Caution urged the young cowboy to back down. Pride insisted he not back down from any man, for any reason.

The two faced each other in deadly silence for several heartbeats. The woman pressed back against the building, her hands flat against the wall, as if trying her best to be invisible. She didn't need to be. Neither man so much as glanced at her.

'I just wanted a kiss,' the cowboy muttered, almost under his breath. Louder, he said, 'We ain't had the last of this.'

Without waiting for a reply he wheeled and strode off in the stiff-legged gait peculiar to those who spent almost every waking hour in a saddle.

Tad turned to the woman. 'Are you OK, ma'am?'

Her eyes darted back and forth between Tad and the retreating cowboy several times. She suddenly became aware of how tightly she was pressed back against the side of the building. She moved her hands, then her whole body away from it. She shot another glance at the front corner of the school, behind which the cowboy had disappeared. She brushed her hands across the front of her skirt as if brushing away some clinging dust or cobwebs.

She took a deep breath and turned to face Tad squarely. Her eyes were surprisingly calm and steady as she looked him in the face. Her voice was as steady as her gaze. 'Yes, I am quite all right. Thank you. I really don't think he intended me any harm. He was just a bit carried away.'

'Somebody you know?'

'I . . . have spoken with him on two or three occasions. Nothing more than that.'

'I think he sorta had his mind set on a bit more than that.'

She ignored the comment. 'Thank you for coming to my rescue. I was afraid he had maneuvered me into too secluded a spot for anyone to do so.'

'I just caught a glimpse of him crowdin' you around the corner,' Tad admitted. 'It didn't look like too good a situation. I thought maybe I'd best check it out.'

'Thank you,' she said yet again. 'I don't think I've seen you in Caldwell City before, have I?'

'No ma'am,' he acknowledged. 'I heard there was some ranches hirin' around here. I'm in need of a job, so I thought I'd check it out.'

Her eyes dropped to the unusually large pistol on his hip, then back to his face. 'Are you a hired gunfighter?' she asked with surprising boldness.

He laughed at the audacity of the question. 'That ain't usually too good a question to ask a stranger,' he suggested.

'I have a habit of speaking my mind,' she replied with no hint of apology. 'Are you?'

'Nope,' he said. 'Not the way that word's usually used, anyway. I've worn a badge a few times, so I guess you could call that being a hired gun, but always and only on the side of the law. Mostly I just try to make an honest livin'. If that means havin' to stand up to someone with a gun, well, sometimes that's just gotta be.'

She studied his gaze for a long moment. Apparently satisfied, she nodded. 'There are ranches hiring. It's not a good time in this country, though. You would do well to be careful to whom you hire your services.'

He was momentarily taken aback by the rarely heard excellence of English. He almost forgot the next sentence he was mentally practicing to say. He recovered quickly. 'Well, that sounds like good advice. Could I offer to buy your supper at whatever Caldwell City boasts for a café, and you can sort out who's who for me.'

The trace of a frown crossed her face. 'Now that was a question, then a statement in the same sentence. Would I require my students to punctuate that with a question mark or a period?'

He chuckled. 'That answers one question. You sure enough gotta be the school teacher.'

She smiled for the first time. The sun seemed to brighten perceptibly as the smile spread across her face, making tiny wrinkles at the corners of her eyes as tiny lights danced within them.

She thrust out a hand. 'My name is Rebecca Folsom. Miss Folsom to my students. Becky to my friends.'

He took the hand and returned its strong, warm grip. 'Does that mean I'm allowed to call you Becky?'

'I think I would like that. And yes, I would be delighted to exchange a supper at Ling Lee's for whatever information I can offer you.'

She led the way, walking with long strides as she chatted easily with him. They had scarcely left the shadow of the school house before he became aware of the layers of trail dust that clung to him. He brushed a hand across three days of stubble on his jaw. 'I'm afraid I ain't too presentable, just comin' off the trail,' he apologized. 'Maybe I'd best get me a room at the hotel and clean up a mite before I try the café.'

She smiled that radiant smile again. 'Don't worry about it. Ling has a water bucket and basin on the porch so working men can wash up before they eat.'

'You forgot the 'r' in warsh,' he teased.

'I'm a school teacher, remember?'

'That's what I mean. A school teacher oughta know there's an 'r' in warsh.'

'Maybe you need to sit in with my third readers for a while.'

'Somehow, I don't think I'd mind that, with you for a teacher,' he responded.

When they reached the café, he washed his hands and face, drying on the roll towel hung beside the wash bench. Without thinking about it, he walked to a table against the back wall. He held the chair with its back toward the dining room for her to be seated. Then he sat down in the chair backed against the wall. He removed his hat and laid it, brim upward, on the floor beside him.

A young Chinese woman appeared at the table. 'Supper, you two?' she asked.

'Yes, please, Lo,' Becky responded.

Lo nodded and wheeled toward the kitchen. 'She and her husband run this place,' she explained to Tad. 'They have very good food. Sometimes I'm not real sure what I'm eating, but it's always delicious.'

Tad changed the subject abruptly. 'You said it's not a good time in this country. Why is that?'

Her eyes grew troubled at once. 'The whole country's on the brink of a range war. There's an awful lot of cattle being stolen. Nobody knows where they're taken. Nobody knows who's doing it. But the ranchers all blame the homesteaders and the little hardscrabble ranchers. The home-steaders think it's an organized band of outlaws, or else big ranchers stealing their own or each other's stock for an excuse to wipe out the little guys. Nobody trusts anyone. Even the kids at school sit 'on their own side' of the room, and stay in groups on the playground to keep from getting beaten up.'

'Sounds bad.'

'It is bad. It's a powder keg. Something's going to happen pretty soon that'll just blow it wide open. I'm not afraid of very many things, but I am really afraid of this situation. Even that half-drunk young cowboy that had me cornered — if it had been one of the homesteaders instead of you that came along, he'd have killed him. Or been killed. And that would have been all it would take to set it all off.'

They ate the surprisingly delicious supper for a while in silence. She walked with him to the livery barn to take care of his horse, then he walked her home. He enjoyed the evening more than any he could ever remember.

As he told her 'good night' at her door, she said, 'Oh, you might try the Flying E Bar, for a job. Ezra Bingham is one of the tough old breed that settled this country, but he's fair and honest, and they say he's good to work for.'

'Thanks,' Tad smiled. 'Where would I find the Flying E Bar?'

Even as he asked the unnecessary question, he felt as if he were somehow betraying her by pretending not to know. That feeling left him puzzled, frowning at himself, as he made his way to the hotel.

3

'Cowpoke Corner Saloon,' Tad muttered to himself as he read the hand-lettered sign on the front of the building. 'Catchy name. Sure lets the sodbusters know they ain't the most welcome folks.'

As he paused inside the door to let his eyes adjust to the lesser light, he noted the abrupt drop in noise level. He felt every eye in the place sizing him up. He walked to the long bar, propped a boot on the well-scarred rail along its front, and responded to the bartender's unspoken question. 'A beer'd taste good if you got one.'

'One beer comin' up,' the bartender nodded.

As he set it in front of Tad and swept the coin off the bar top, he said, 'Ain't seen you here before.'

'Just rode in a while ago,' Tad

responded. He carefully kept his voice light, conversational. 'Looks like a nice town. Seems sorta well churched, though.'

The bartender grinned in response. 'You think it's well churched now. You oughta hear how well on a Sunday mornin' when you're nursin' a hang-over.'

Tad chuckled as well. 'I thought of that when I saw them bells. They ring 'em at the same time?'

The bartender nodded. 'Same time, an' neither one wants to quit till the other one quits first. I swear they clang them things for fifteen minutes some-times.'

'Well, I guess nobody can say they missed church 'cause they overslept, thataway.'

The bartender nodded. He leaned forward across the bar. His voice lowered as if imparting some privileged information. 'Somebody slipped around and cut both bell ropes one Saturday night a while back.'

Tad laughed. 'I bet that caused a stir.'

'Yeah, you might call it that. Kinda like turnin' over a shovel full o' dirt in an ant hill. I thought them gentle church-goin' folks was gonna lynch the town marshal for lettin' somethin' that heinous happen.'

The bartender moved away to tend to other customers, leaving Tad to study the occupants of the saloon in the mirror behind the bar. The noise level had risen back almost to the level it was when he first entered. Most of the tables of men had returned to their conversations, their card games, their flirting with one or more of the 'working girls,' or their serious drinking.

One table was a clear exception. Four cowboys at that table continued to watch him. They talked to each other, but without taking their eyes from him. It was obvious he was the topic of their conversation.

'In about ten more minutes,' Tad told himself, 'the fella with the short straw's gonna come over and start askin' questions.'

He was wrong. It took only half that time.

One of the cowboys came to his feet. He was exceptionally broad-shouldered. His bulging shoulders crowded the capacity of his shirt to accommodate them. From those shoulders, his torso tapered to hips that were as unusually narrow as his shoulders were broad. 'Fast as a cat, and stouter than a bull,' Tad told himself.

The cowboy strode to the bar, leaning on it about three feet away from Tad. 'New in Caldwell, ain't you?'

Tad was very well aware how much most people resemble a mirror. Most folks tend to respond in the same way they are addressed. If they are addressed in anger, they will respond in anger. If they are approached with open friendliness, it's very difficult for them to respond in an opposite manner. He often used that knowledge to his decided advantage.

He responded to the question with what was almost an overly friendly grin. He thrust a hand toward the inquisitive cowboy. 'That I am. Name's Tad Strong.'

The unexpected affability took the cowboy by surprise, making his response a couple heartbeats slower than it would have normally been. He took the extended hand as if there were no other possible response, and returned the firm handshake. 'Uh, Luther Summers,' he responded.

'You ride for one of the ranches around here?'

Clearly taken aback by Tad's open and ready friendliness, he again hesitated slightly before responding. Tad kept himself from smiling as he noted the effect of keeping the young cowhand off balance. 'Yeah. Yeah, I do. I ride for the Flyin' E Bar.'

'They hirin'?' Tad queried instantly.

After the repeated heartbeat of hesitation, he replied, 'Uh, well, I guess I don't rightly know. You lookin' to hire on somewhere?'

'Yeah, I sure do need a job,' Tad responded. 'Ain't gonna be long afore my backbone decides my throat's been cut, if I don't find one. Are there very many outfits hirin' that you know of?'

The cowboy visibly fought to force himself away from the defensive position Tad's surprising friendliness had put him in. Grasping to take the initiative again, his voice took on a more decisive, almost belligerent tone, totally ignoring Tad's last question. 'We been watchin' you since you come in. You strike us as more of a gunman than a cowpoke.'

'That so?' Tad affected a surprised expression. 'Now what would make you think that?'

'You wear that big oversized hogleg like you'd rather handle it than a rope or a sick steer, for one thing.'

'Naw. Not unless I need to, anyway,' Tad replied. 'Can't say I really like havin' to use it.'

'I ain't sure I believe that,' Luther

argued. 'We're thinkin' you've likely been hired by them sodbusters, and came in here to see if you could stir stuff up, and maybe crowd some reg'lar cowhand into gunplay.'

Tad dropped the appearance of overt friendliness. His eyes bored into the young ranch hand. 'Have you seen me crowdin' anybody?'

The young man didn't back down at all. He appeared, rather, to welcome the challenge in Tad's eyes. 'We ain't aimin' to wait to give you the chance. Instead of waitin' to let you pick out somebody slow and awkward, I'm beatin' you to the punch. If you're lookin' for trouble, you can start out by tryin' me on for size.'

As he spoke, Luther stepped back away from the bar. His hand dropped to brush lightly against the butt of his pistol. Tad deliberately looked him up and down. He just as deliberately turned back to the bar. He leaned forward, resting both forearms on the polished surface. 'Nah, I got no reason to do that,' he dismissed the cowboy. 'I'm lookin' for a job, not a fight.'

Frustration and irritation took turns crossing Luther's face. He glanced at the table where his friends watched, then back at Tad. He shook his head slightly. 'I think you are,' he argued. 'Just not with me. I think you'd jump at the chance with someone you're sure you could beat.'

With a sigh Tad straightened from the bar. 'If I was lookin' for a fight, you'd do just fine,' he said, keeping his voice carefully light. 'If I was lookin' for a fight, I'd kill you before you could get that gun half way out of its holster.'

That was the challenge Luther was waiting for. His body tensed in anticipation. 'If you think so, why don't you go for that gun of your — '

The last letter of his challenge was cut short by the barrel of Tad's .44 pressing against the end of his nose. He hadn't seen Tad move. He hadn't realized the stranger even intended to draw yet. He hadn't even had a chance to grip the handle of his own gun, let alone pull it from its holster.

Instant silence descended on the room. Every eye watched in stunned wonder. Several jaws hung in open amazement. Luther's face drained of color. His eyes crossed as he stared at the gunbarrel pressing against the end of his nose. He carefully moved his hands outward, away from his body.

His eyes jerked up to meet Tad's calm gaze, then crossed again as he stared at the gunbarrel in his face.

Tad's voice was conciliatory. 'Like I said, son, if I was lookin' for a fight, you'd be well advised to avoid me, not to call me out. But I ain't. I'm just as good with horses or as a cowhand as I am with this weapon. I'm lookin' for a job, where I can just be a cowboy. Would that be OK with you?'

Luther started to nod, then thought better of moving his head. His eyes darted to meet Tad's, then back to the gunbarrel. 'Yeah. Yeah, sure. I didn't mean . . . damn! I ain't never even heard of anybody that fast with a gun.'

As swiftly as it had appeared against his nose, the gun disappeared. Luther blinked. The gun was back in its holster, and Tad's hand was no place near it. He swallowed audibly. Color returned to his face, and didn't know when to stop. He turned as red as he had been ashen moments before. He stammered as he spoke. 'You . . . I . . . damn! You'da killed me slicker'n a whistle if you'da wanted to. I . . . uh . . . guess I owe you a thanks. Uh, sorry I braced you thataway.'

Tad carefully steered the conversation to lower the level of tension in the room. 'Everybody seems plumb jumpy and suspicious. Somethin' goin' on around here?'

Luther grasped the opportunity eagerly. He nodded. 'There's been a whole lot o' trouble brewin' for a while. Everybody's losin' stock in pretty big bunches.'

Tad frowned as if hearing the fact for the first time. 'Is that so? Where's it goin'?'

'Nobody knows for sure. We figger it's the homesteaders, cuttin' our herds down so's we won't crowd the plowed fields they're tryin' to fence off. Ruinin' the range is what they're doin'. The sodbusters claim it's us, just lookin' for an excuse to run 'em outa the country. Nobody seems to find any proof either way. Anybody that tries too hard ends up dead all of a sudden.'

Tad pursed his lips thoughtfully. 'Don't sound good. Not what I was hopin' to find, when I heard there were outfits around here hirin'.'

'It ain't a good situation to ride into,' Luther agreed.

He glanced at the table where his friends sat, unsure of how to continue. 'Uh, like I said, I, uh, ain't sure my outfit's hirin' right now. But if you're in fact lookin' for an honest job, you might try Grunt anyway. If you're sure on the up and up, I'd put in a word for you.'

'Grunt?' Tad echoed, as if the name were new to him. 'That your foreman?'

Luther shook his head. 'Nah, he's the owner. His name's Ezra Bingham. We just call 'im Grunt.'

Tad turned his gaze toward the table from which Luther had risen. He raised his voice just a little, keeping its tone as casual as possible. 'Any of you boys object if I ride out and see if your boss needs another hand?'

Obviously surprised at the question, the trio remaining at the table exchanged hurried looks before returning their gazes to Tad. One of them finally said, 'Well, no, I 'spect not.'

Another chimed in instantly. 'I'm plumb sure we'd a whole lot rather have you workin' with us than agin us.'

One of the trio laughed abruptly at the words. 'You got that right!' he enthused in the sudden release of tension. 'Dang, you're good with that gun! Can you shoot as straight as you are quick?'

Tad grinned as if he'd been asked a completely innocuous question. 'Naw, not really. I missed what I was shootin' at once, no more than seven or eight months ago. Of course, a hundred yards is kinda outa range for a .44.'

Two of the three grinned in response to the light-hearted answer. The one who had spoken said, 'Well, then, you'd just as well come on over and have a drink with us. I'm Dutch.'

'You look it, all right,' Tad agreed. 'What's your name?'

There was just an instant of silence before those at the table caught it, then they all laughed just a little louder than natural.

Tad elbowed himself away from the bar and followed Luther to the table. Dutch pulled an extra chair from a nearby table and motioned to it. Tad took the chair, aware he was exposing his back to part of the room. Even so, he was confident that the native, open honesty of the cowhands rendered them incapable of drawing him into that position for any reasons of treachery.

He was a good judge of character. He fully enjoyed the next hour of conversation.

4

It might have been any of a hundred places in the sparsely settled western frontier. Nestled near the head of Grand Valley, the snow-capped peaks of the Absaroka Mountain chain towered in the distance. Numerous mountain streams, fed by springs and snow melt tumbled musically over rocks and defiles. When they encountered gentler slopes, they were deterred in their downward flow by dozens of beaver dams. Those amazing structures did more than slow the water's flow. In so doing, they also spread the life-giving moisture across broad expanses. It was they that made every mountain meadow a veritable paradise of wild flowers, tall grass, and future forests. Wildlife in abundance grazed placidly with the herds of cattle.

The ranch yard itself was arranged in

a manner that seemed, somehow, rigidly prescribed. Built during a time when the primary objective was simply to survive, it was built with the obvious hope of better and more prosperous days. The front porch of the house looked out across a wide yard, with the barn, corrals, bunkhouse, cookhouse and blacksmith shop forming a rough semicircle that marked the far side of the yard.

Hinged shutters were fastened open at the sides of every window in the ranch house. Each sported rifle slots in the form of a cross in the center. They bore mute testimony to the unsettled times in which the ranches were founded. More than a few of those houses showed the slivered and pitted evidence of bullets, arrows, or both. They bore mute testimony that such precautions were well warranted.

The yard of the Flying E Bar might have been any one of those sites. There was little to distinguish it. It was, perhaps, more meticulously maintained than most. Every post was straight. Every door hung true and swung easily. There were no sagging or broken rails on the corrals. Every building, including the barn, had windows of real glass. No trash or litter was visible. All the small brush was carefully cleared in a hundred-yard circle around the buildings. If trouble came, it wouldn't be allowed to sneak up close to the buildings unseen. Neither could a wildfire overrun the buildings, deprived as it would be of fuel in their immediate vicinity.

The buildings were set near the top of a long slope, far enough from the summit to be sheltered from winter winds, yet high enough to provide a majestic view of the valley stretching eastward.

Tad took in the details of house and yard approvingly. Four dogs announced his arrival when he was scarcely through the gate that approached it. In response, Ezra Bingham stepped out onto the porch. He yelled something

46

unintelligible, and the dogs ceased their barking.

'Mornin',' Ezra called as Tad approached. 'Nice day.'

'Sure is,' Tad called back. 'Nice place you got here.'

'We like it.'

'You hirin'?'

'Well, we're always lookin' to hire good hands. You any good?'

Tad grinned. 'Well, that depends on who you ask, I 'spect. I can handle stock as good as most. I'm stout, honest, not afraid of work, and I never bellyache about the coffee.'

Ezra grinned in response. 'Well, that'd set you apart from every other hand I got. Get down. I'll take you over to the cookhouse and see if you can get a whole cup down without breakin' that promise. It'll be up to Oz to hire you on or not. He's my foreman.'

Maintaining the appearance of never having met before, Ezra took Tad to the cookhouse. He called to an old Mexican hand, whose job was obviously maintenance of buildings and yard, to fetch Oscar Peterson, the foreman.

As they entered the cookhouse, Tad instantly recognized two cowboys sitting together at the other end of the long table. A flicker of recognition flashed in both of their eyes, as well as his. It was two of the trio who had witnessed his confrontation with Luther at the saloon. He waited for a reaction from them, but both chose to show no recognition of him.

They were scarcely seated at the long table in the cookhouse, promised cup of strong coffee in hand, when Oscar arrived. He appraised Tad with a quick, hard look up and down the length of his body, then turned to his boss. 'You sent for me, Grunt?'

Ezra nodded. 'Oz, this here's . . . well danged if I didn't forget to even ask your name.'

Tad grinned. 'Tad Strong.' As he spoke, he extended a hand to the foreman. 'Lookin' for work.'

Oscar took the proffered hand in the

customary tight grip, looking Tad in the eyes intently. 'You any good?'

Tad laughed. 'Now that's twice inside of an hour I been asked that question.'

Ezra broke in. 'He says he can ride, rope, shoot, and tell tall tales even better'n you can, Oz.'

Oscar snorted. 'You'd just as well ride out, then. Can't have anyone like that on the place. I don't mind bein' out-ridden, out-roped and out-shot, but danged if I'll tolerate a bigger liar in the bunkhouse. And that's the truth if I ever told it.'

Tad scratched the back of his neck, as if in deep thought. 'Well, I 'spect I could keep it toned down enough to not show you up any.'

Oscar extended a hand, palm up. 'Mind if I take a look at that hogleg?'

Instinctively, Tad's hand dropped to brush the well-worn walnut grips. His eyes darted from Oscar to Ezra and back to Oscar. From the corner of his eye he noted the jerk of surprise from both cowboys at the other end of the table. He saw them look at each other, then fix their gazes back on him. Reluctantly, he slid the weapon from its holster. Reversing it almost awkwardly, he handed it, butt first, to the foreman.

A flicker of surprise crossed Ezra's face before he masked it. Oscar took the gun, keeping it carefully pointed away from either of the other men. He checked the loads, noting the hammer rested on the only empty chamber in the nine-round cylinder. The gun was meticulously clean, well cared for, perfectly oiled, with no excess oil residue on its surface.

Oscar nodded his satisfaction. He handed it back to Tad. Tad dropped it into its holster, trying his best to mask the intense relief its return flooded through him. 'You're hired,' Oscar announced. 'Thirty an' found. Five horses for your string. All the ammunition you need. Anything you need from town, tallied against whatever time you got comin'. Five days off to go to town every three months to blow off steam and get rid of your wages, if you're a mind to.'

'Fair enough,' Tad agreed, not mentioning the conflicting agreement he and Ezra had already established. 'What was the deal with my gun?'

Oscar grinned. 'Little foible o' mine. If you're careless at all, it'll show up in the way you take care of your hogleg. If you're a gunfighter, you'll be packin' a short-barreled one that'll draw quick. Probably small caliber, 'cause they're lighter and quicker. And if you're a gunfighter, it'd be a cold day in hell when you'd hand it over to a stranger thataway. A man that packs a piece that big an' heavy is a man that believes in bein' prepared for most anything, and believes in gettin' a job done. I ain't never seen a handgun that big afore, though. What is it?'

'Russian .44.'

'Lot o' fire power.'

'It generally gets the job done.'

'You want your horses from the rough string or the gentler ones?'

Tad's eyebrows rose slightly. This man never ceased to surprise him. 'I'd rather not have to ride too hard every time I get on one,' he said honestly. 'I don't mind a horse crow-hoppin' of a mornin', but I like to know he ain't gonna blow up on me in the middle o' somethin', or if a rabbit busts outa the brush.'

Oz nodded his agreement. 'I'll have the wrangler corral some for you to check out first thing in the mornin'.'

'Fair enough.'

He turned to Ezra and began asking questions about cattle and what men would be sent where the next day, indicating he was finished with the new hand. Tad finished the cup of coffee, and shuddered involuntarily with the bitter aftertaste of its being too long on the stove.

The shudder didn't go entirely unnoticed. 'Thought you wasn't gonna complain,' Ezra reminded him, tongue in cheek.

'I didn't say a word,' Tad protested.

One of the cowboys at the other end of the table spoke for the first time. 'He would've, I bet, but he took a big swallow. After that he couldn't say nothin' till he quit shudderin'.'

'His eyes didn't cross none, though,' the other hand observed. 'He just may be tough enough to survive Hank's cookin'.'

'Watch your tongue or you won't,' came an unexpected voice from the kitchen.

'Oh, sorry, Hank!' the cowboy grinned. 'I didn't have any idea you might be listenin' out there.'

'You'll know it when supper time comes,' Hank's voice threatened.

The two stood. The last speaker walked over and extended a hand to Tad. 'I'm Verle Dutcher. Folks just call me 'Dutch'.' He waved a hand in the direction of his companion. 'This here's Ike Kilmer. C'mon. I'll take you over to the bunkhouse and show you which empties are farthest from Ike's. He snores like a bull moose with a bellyache and a head cold. The farther you bunk from him, the better chance you got of gettin' a little bit of sleep.'

They were scarcely out the door of the cook house when Dutch confronted him. 'You wanta tell me what's goin' on?'

'Whatd'ya mean?'

'You know dang well what I mean. You're the fastest man with a gun I ever seen in my life, and you let on like you ain't no gunman at all. You fixin' to put one over on the boss? If you are, I'll do my dangdest to stop your clock, even if you kill me for it.'

'Good for you,' Tad surprised him by saying. He looked Dutch up and down. He made the snap decision to trust the cowboy, partially because he didn't see much choice. 'Ezra knows better. I 'spect Oz does too, but he wasn't tippin' his hand, so I didn't either. The fact is, Ezra looked me up in Cheyenne, and hired me. I was sportin' a badge at the time. I was hired to find out who's behind all the rustlin', and put a stop to it. We figured it'd be best for the time bein' if nobody knows that's why I'm here. I'd sort of appreciate it if you boys'd keep it that way for a while.'

Dutch looked him over carefully again before responding. Finally he nodded. 'That ain't gonna be easy, though. Me, Ike, Joe and Luther been spendin' most of our bunkhouse time rehashin' what you did to Luther in town. As soon as the boys figure out that was you, they'll know somethin's fishy. They'll figure it out quick enough, too. There ain't none of us seen a hogleg like that afore, and the chances is somewhere betwixt slim an' none that two of 'em would show up in the country at the same time. You might be better off trustin' 'em than tryin' to pull the wool over their eyes.'

Tad saw the wisdom of the advice instantly. 'Can they all be trusted?'

Dutch shrugged. He took a long, thoughtful breath. 'I'm guessin' they can. You never know for sure, but they all been here a long while. Grunt don't lose hands as quick as most places. I think every man on the place'll ride for the brand to hell an' back. There ain't a man ridin' for Grunt that's been with 'im less than three years. 'Ceptin' you, that is.'

'How many are there?'

'Eleven. Twelve now, countin' you.'

'That count Oscar?'

'Yup. He's the straw boss, but he's one o' the boys. Stays in the bunkhouse like the rest of us.'

'Good man?'

'The best. And you can bet your buttons Grunt told him who you are and why you're here. That makes six outa the twelve, countin' you again, that already know. Like I said, part of the stories we been tellin' about you was that oversized hogleg of yours. The other boys is gonna put two an' two together in a hurry. There ain't another man in the country packin' a gun like that.'

'Then go ahead and let 'em know what the deal is,' Tad agreed. 'Ask 'em to keep it to themselves, though. No sense gettin' me bushwhacked too quick.'

He had the distinct feeling that it wouldn't take long for someone to try anyway.

5

Tad stepped effortlessly into his well-worn saddle. As his right boot found the off stirrup, the big bay gelding tossed his head slightly, took two steps forward, then began to buck half-heartedly, working the morning kinks from his well-muscled body. He crow-hopped half a dozen jumps, then Tad's spurs poked him lightly in the sides. He responded instantly. At full speed in three jumps, he was across the corral in seconds. At the last minute Tad pulled one way on the reins, leaning that way simultaneously. Without slowing, the horse swapped ends and lunged across the corral the other direction. They did that several times, with Tad indicating his will for the horse to turn first left, then right, then right, then left again. He hauled the horse to a stop with a nod of satisfaction.

He reached down and patted the side of the gelding's neck appreciatively. The horse tossed his head a couple times, indicating his willingness to continue the exercise. 'Good horse,' he said as he nodded toward the wrangler watching from the top rail of the corral. 'They all this good, Lyle?'

The wrangler glanced toward the other four horses awaiting his assessment in the adjoining corral. 'Oh, all 'cept the bay mare, I'd say. She's a fine horse, but a mite spookier'n the others. She ain't never blowed up with me since she was good an' broke, but she still shies a little when a prairie hen jumps up, or a rabbit takes off, or somethin' like that.'

They were interrupted by Oz Peterson, riding up on the big black mare he favored. 'You mind checkin' the others out in a day or two?' he asked Tad.

Tad's eyebrows shot up. 'No, I guess not. What's up?'

'I just thought I'd ride out with you myself today, sorta show you the lay o' the ranch a little bit. Let you know what we expect from a hand. If that gelding suits you, just come ahead and ride him today, and we'll get started.'

'Sure,' Tad agreed. 'I'll ride by the bunkhouse and grab the stuff I like to keep with me.'

Oz nodded. He was offering some instructions to Lyle Wingaard, the wrangler, as Tad rode out of the corral and headed for the bunkhouse.

Fifteen minutes later he and Oz left the yard at a swift trot. As they rode, Oz offered a running commentary on the lay of the land, how far in each direction the Flying E Bar's holdings ran, how many head of cattle they were supposed to have, how much of the land was deeded or filed on, how much was free range, and brief interjections of the history of the area.

'Are we lookin' for somethin' in particular today?' Tad asked finally.

Oz glanced sideways, measuring him carefully before answering. 'Never know,' he evaded. 'We got a bunch o' fine steers gettin' close to market size, that I been frettin' about some. They're a prime mark for rustlers. I been keepin' a pretty close eye on 'em.'

'Have you thought any of campin' out where you can keep watch on 'em?'

'Thought about it,' Oz confirmed. 'Just didn't wanta leave one man alone to do it. He'd likely get hisself killed if the rustlers did show up. Can't spare three or four to watch one bunch. Besides, that many'd be hard to keep hid.'

'But you think they're about ready to hit this bunch?'

Oz shrugged, shifting in the saddle. 'Well, I would, if I was them. That's about all I know to go on.'

'Good a hunch as any,' Tad agreed.

'Besides, I wanted to get off where we could talk without the other hands overhearin'. I ain't had a chance to ask you how much you want them knowin'.'

Tad nodded approvingly. 'I appreciate that,' he replied. 'They know who I am and why I'm here, though.'

Oz 's eyebrows shot up. 'They do?'

Tad nodded. 'I sorta had a run-in with Luther in town. Sorta stuck my gun barrel up his nose to convince him I wasn't a ringer sent in by the sodbusters or the rustlers.'

Oz grinned. 'Now that I'da like to've seen. What happened?'

'Oh, he cooled off right quick. Then I visited with him and Dutch and Ike and Joe a while. I acted like it was on their say-so I rode out and applied for a job.'

'Then how do they know why you're here?'

'Well, they dang well knew I was a better gun hand than you let on like you was thinkin'. That, and I just don't like the boys I may have to depend on bein' kept in the dark, like I don't trust 'em. They all been with you quite a while. If there was a rustler in the bunch, they'd likely know it. I told 'em what the deal was, and asked 'em to keep it to themselves. I'm guessin' they will.'

Oz mulled it over in his mind for

quite a while before he answered. 'Yeah, I 'spect they will, all right. We got a good crew.'

It was almost two hours later when both men simultaneously jerked their horses to a halt. Both cocked their head sideways, listening intently. Faintly, borne on the light breeze from the far side of the hill, they heard it again. Somebody yipped and barked, the unmistakable sound of cowboys driving cattle.

Tad looked at the foreman. 'Would them be your cattle bein' driven?'

'Couldn't be nobody else's, over here in this part o' the valley. Gotta be them steers I was worryin' about.'

'Headin' south, sound like. Is there a good spot up ahead we can get to without 'em seein' or hearin' us, where we might surprise 'em a bit?'

Lips tight in a combination of anger and jubilation, Oz nodded. 'Just over a mile ahead, if they keep goin' the direction they are, they gotta go through a broad swale, maybe three hundred yards across. From up on the sides, we'd have a pretty good view o' things.'

'Any cover?'

'Lots o' scrub cedar on the slopes for us. Pertneart none in the bottom for them.'

'Can't get much better'n that. Lead the way.'

With no more conversation, Oz swerved his horse away from the noises. When he judged them to be sufficiently away from the unseen rustlers, he kicked his horse to a run, leaning low over the saddle horn. Tad's horse followed without instruction, keeping pace with the other mount.

The horses were nearly at the limit of their ability to run flat out when Oz reined in. They sat on the top of a ridge that dropped gently to a broad swale. There, the rough, broken country offered a wide, relatively smooth avenue, almost as if a road had led through there in some far-off time. Small clumps of scrub cedar dotted the side hills, but the bottom of the wide draw was free of trees and brush.

'Couldn't ask for anything better,' Tad repeated his previous assessment.

'You want this side or the other?'

'I'll take the other.'

'You gonna give 'em a chance to give themselves up?'

Tad's jaw clamped hard, knotting the muscle at the jaws' hinges. He shook his head. 'I don't guess we'd really have to.' His voice betrayed his discomfort with the logic of his own words, as if trying to convince himself. 'If they're drivin' your steers, there ain't no question they're rustlers. If they surrender, we'll hang 'em, and they know it. We'd be well within our rights to just open up on 'em right off the bat. Still and yet . . .'

'Yeah, I can't argue with you,' Oz agreed. 'Still and yet it goes against my grain to just open up on somebody without even givin' 'em a chance to give it up.'

The contrary options hung in the still

air as if being turned and examined by all sides by both men. Both already knew which option they would choose. The unspoken honor of the country simply demanded it.

Without giving voice to the unspoken decision, Oz said, 'I'll set up behind that cedar right over there.'

'I'll set up behind that one straight across the draw,' Tad motioned. 'You'll know right off if they're your steers. If they are, it'll be up to you to open the festivities. I'll open up as soon as you do.'

Ten minutes later both men were in place. Their horses were tethered well out of sight, over the crest of the rise, where they wouldn't be spotted by the rustlers.

In addition to his pistol, Tad was armed with a .44/.40 rifle. A full box of shells lay open on the ground at his feet. Another unopened box lay beside it. Lying to one side, but within easy reach, was also a .50 caliber Sharps rifle. Extra shells for it lay on the ground for easy access as well.

It was only minutes before they heard the first sounds of the approaching cattle and herders. As they came into sight, Tad's eyes widened. 'They're takin' over a hundred head at a time,' he muttered. 'They're either mighty greedy or cock-sure they ain't gonna have trouble gettin' rid of 'em.'

He counted nine rustlers driving the steers. 'Pretty poor odds if we didn't have the cover and the surprise both,' Tad observed. He took a deep, thoughtful breath. 'Pretty poor odds anyway,' he admitted.

He waited with increasing nervousness. He guessed when the closest of the rustlers were well within range, anticipating Oz's challenge. No such sound disturbed the serenity of the pastoral setting.

The lead riders were almost between him and Oz when the foreman finally spoke. From behind the cover of the cedar he yelled, 'Throw up your hands! You're surrounded.'

Response from the outlaws was instant. Before Oz even finished his sentence, bark and needles were flying from the cedar around him. With no more hesitation he fired in response.

Before the sound of his rifle reached Tad, the first of the rustlers flung both hands in the air and flopped backward out of the saddle.

Tad's first shot was so swift behind the evidence of that first shot that the sound of Oz's rifle was drowned out by the roar of his own. A second rustler grunted and doubled forward, then tumbled from the saddle.

Return fire from the rustlers raked the cedars, even before any of them sought cover. By the time any of them decided to dive behind some form of protection, two more of their number were on the ground, dead or dying.

Reaction by the remaining five was swift and practiced, however. Two of them dove from their horses, scrambling behind rocks and brush for whatever cover they could find. The two farthest from the hidden rifles wheeled their horses and spurred them frantically, fleeing as fast as their mounts would carry them.

The fifth of the survivors drove his horse straight for Tad's cover, firing his rifle with amazing speed and precision, pinning Tad behind the branches of the cedar. A round from Oz's rifle spun him in the saddle, but failed to unseat him.

Even wounded, he whirled to that side and fired at his new attacker, missing Oz by scant inches. A bullet from Tad's rifle knocked him from the saddle an instant later. He was dead before he hit the ground.

A steady hail of bullets shattered branches and chipped bark from the cedars that sheltered both men. Ignoring it, but staying as well protected as he could, Tad laid the .44/.40 down and picked up the Sharps. He lay flat on the ground with the big rifle cradled on a branch scant inches from the dirt. Sighting at the first of the fleeing drag riders, he squeezed the trigger. The roar of the large-caliber weapon silenced the return fire of the two partially concealed rustlers for a full second.

When the force of the .50-caliber leaden slug drove one of the fleeing rustlers down onto his saddle horn, Tad was already lining his sights on the other. He was driven from the saddle an instant later by an identical leaden ball of death.

The gunfire from the pinned down rustlers resumed instantly. A responding shot from Oz's rifle was followed by the unmistakable thwack of a bullet finding soft flesh.

Eschewing the smaller-caliber weapon, Tad trained the Sharps on the brush directly in front of the lone remaining, still invisible, gunman. The massive slug of the buffalo gun tore through the brush and grass without the distortion of its trajectory the smaller weapon would have experienced. It found the unseen rustler as if guided by some unseen force, abruptly ending his unlawful career.

Deathly silence settled over the bloody vista. The cattle, at the first volley of shots, had whirled and thundered back the way they had come. Slowed now to a walk and scattering, they continued to move back toward the familiar range from which they had been driven.

The rustlers' horses, likewise, had spooked and run a short ways. Each was now placidly tearing off mouthfuls of the tall grass, oblivious to the deaths of their owners.

'You OK, Oz?' Tad called.

'I'll make it,' Oz replied.

Concern instantly flooded Tad's face, tinging his voice with concern. 'You get hit?'

'Yeah, I got nicked. Ripped a chunk outa my side. Bleedin' pretty good, but it didn't even bust the rib, I don't think.'

Tad retrieved his horse and hurried across the swale to check out the wound for himself. By the time he got there, the foreman had already ripped strips of cotton fabric from a sleeve of his underwear, and had tied it around his body. It had stanched the flow of blood, and he was already putting his shirt back on.

'Pretty hard on underwear, ain't you?' Tad offered.

'Saves havin' to warsh 'em,' Oz rejoined instantly. 'Gives me a chance to be one o' them rich guys that just throws 'em away when they get dirty. You're leakin' a mite o' blood yourself.'

Tad swiped a hand across his face, noticing for the first time the tickle of small rivulets of blood making their way down both sides of his face. 'Just slivers off that cedar, I think,' he said.

He pulled his shirt tail from his trousers and used it to wipe the blood from his face. He felt gingerly around his face, noting the half dozen small gouges that flying fragments of cedar had ripped in his skin. From one of them he extracted a pointed piece of wood nearly an inch long. 'You got a couple pretty good gouges yourself,' he observed. 'If there's cedar berries plowed in there, you may have a tree or two growin' outa your face next month.'

'Well, if it does, at least I'll have somethin' handy to make toothpicks out of,' Oz observed, dabbing at the blood on his own face and arm.

Tad became serious again almost at once. 'What do you wanta do with them fellas?'

Oz pursed his lips thoughtfully. 'Tie 'em on their horses and send 'em home, I 'spect,' he suggested. 'I'd like to see where they go home to.'

'That's what I was thinkin',' Tad agreed. 'You hold the horses while I tie 'em over their saddles, then I'll follow 'em while you ride back to the place.'

'That ain't too smart, followin' 'em all by yourself.'

'I'll stay back a ways,' Tad promised. 'I oughta be able to tell where they go without gettin' myself in a jam.'

Oz's expression reflected the same doubts Tad was trying hard to ignore.

6

The violent deaths of men never sets well on any land. Even the elements seem to react. The sun covered its face from the slaughter. Cringing behind the cover of great thunderheads it slunk beyond the western mountains to regain its composure. But, like the men beneath it, it would retreat for the night, then rise again tomorrow as if the previous day's violence were of little moment.

In the soft light between its departure and the encroaching darkness, a macabre procession of death-laden horses plodded, heads down, along the main street of a town called Churchville. None of the nine horses playing follow-the-leader noticed nor cared that a cautious rider trailed them at a distance, keeping carefully out of sight.

They were half way down the

primary street of Churchville, just passing The Pleasure Emporium, Churchville's elaborate, but sole, saloon and whorehouse, when the first cry of alarm rang out.

That first shout was followed by half a dozen more, then by the thunder of two-dozen pairs of boots. Hands grabbed the tied-back reins of cow ponies turned funerary biers. Names were shouted up and down the street, identifying the dead men.

The door of The Pleasure Emporium whipped open with a force that threatened the grip of its hinges. A giant of a man glowered from beneath a thatch of red hair that escaped the cover of the large Stetson pushed back from his forehead. Moving with a grace and speed that belied his size, he bellowed, 'What's goin' on out here?'

Men instantly moved aside to make way for him. He stopped stock still, staring incredulously at what he would have gambled impossible. The import of what he saw slowly registered. 'All nine of 'em?' he growled finally.

'All nine,' a lone voice affirmed hesitantly.

'Shot or hung?'

'All shot. Two in the back, like they was tryin' to get away.'

'Any notes on 'em?'

'Nope.'

'Anyone followin' 'em?'

Close enough to hear the exchange, Tad Strong shrank back into the murky shadows between two buildings. He felt the probing of dozens of eyes scanning the street, prying into its dark corners. There was no answer to the big man's query for several seconds. Finally a venturous voice offered, 'Didn't see nobody, Burly.'

Another reticent fellow found his voice. 'Nobody'd be dumb enough to follow 'em all the way here, Burly.'

Bertram Bligh turned the full force of his gaze on the speaker. 'You'da told me nobody could take on this bunch and win, too, wouldn't you?'

The man he addressed swallowed

hard, suddenly studying the toes of his boots. His voice carried far less assurance as he replied, 'Well, yeah. Yeah, I sure would've. These boys was all mighty good hands with a gun.'

'Then whatd'ya s'pose happened?' Bligh demanded.

The hapless focus of the big man's wrath shrugged uncomfortably. 'Danged if I got any idea, Burly. Somebody musta had an ambush set up for 'em. Had to've been a whole bunch of 'em, though.'

'Then maybe we'd best be findin' out who an' how,' Burly opined.

Murmurs of agreement drifted from all parts of the street. Burly jabbed a finger at three men in succession. 'Rusty, Panhandle, Wilson. You three take a couple days. Ride over to Caldwell City. Poke around wherever else you're a mind to. See who's goin' to funerals, an' who's talkin'. These boys dang sure didn't check out without takin' someone with 'em. If you find the funerals, you'll find out who set it up.'

Wordlessly, the trio wheeled and headed for the livery barn to collect their horses and gear.

The big man jabbed his finger at a long, lean man clad in buckskins. 'Arapaho, you backtrack 'em. See what you can find out.'

The man he called 'Arapaho' nodded wordlessly. He slid silently away, seeming not to even move the air around him as he glided down the street.

Burly turned on his heel and started back toward the door of the Pleasure Emporium. A voice from the crowd in the street stopped him in his tracks. 'Whatd'ya want us to do with these boys, Burly?'

Bligh whirled and faced the direction of the anonymous speaker. His eyes flashed. His jaw muscles bulged. His head jutted forward. He singled the speaker out from among his fellows and fixed a scorching glare on him. 'Whatd'ya usually do with dead men, Stinky? Since you don't seem to know, it's high time you find out. You bury 'em. By yourself.'

Nobody dared breathe for a long moment. Stinky's voice turned plaintive. 'There's nine of 'em, Burly! I'll be diggin' graves all night!'

'Make dang sure they're done before sunup or somebody'll be diggin' yours,' he threatened.

A lean, dark, pinch-faced gunman chuckled unexpectedly. Addressing Bligh, he said, 'I guess your boys wasn't near as good as you thought they were, huh Burly?'

Quick as a cat's blink, Bligh's gun was in his fist, spouting fire from its muzzle. Before the insolent gunman had any idea he was in danger, the first slug from Bligh's .45 buried itself in his chest. Every bullet from the Colt's cylinder found flesh in the already dead gunman before his body settled on the ground.

Jaw muscles bulged, teeth clenched, Bligh's eyes glared at every watching man in turn. Nothing moved. Nobody spoke. Silence reigned up and down the street as Bligh replaced the spent loads from his sidearm and returned it to its holster. Only then did he speak. 'Stinky! Make it ten.'

He turned, thrusting his weight back through the door of the saloon. From within, his voice could be clearly heard calling to one of the women in his employ. 'Sadie! I need some company. I'm some upset. Come make me forget how mad it makes me to lose that many men.'

Nobody offered to give Stinky a hand.

Stinky led away the horses bearing their dead weights. As if that were some kind of signal, most of the neck-craners in the street funneled back into The Pleasure Emporium. Two of their number finally looked at one another, shrugged, and stooped together to lift the body of the hapless victim of Bligh's wrath, following Stinky's reluctant path to the hill on the edge of town.

When the street was empty and silent, Tad slowly, carefully worked his way back to his horse. Leading the animal quietly out of town, he stepped into the saddle and rode swiftly away.

★   ★   ★

Daylight found him striding up to the door of Becky Folsom's house in Caldwell City. He started to knock on the door, then thought better of it. In a soft voice he called, 'Becky, are you up yet?'

The door opened almost instantly. The smell of coffee and frying bacon triggered an instant surge of hunger. The sight of Becky, obviously dressed for a day of teaching, roused a different hunger in him, just as intense.

Surprise and undisguised delight brought a radiant smile to her face. 'Tad! What are you doing in town so early? Come on in.' Intruding thoughts tempered the smile with sudden concern. 'Are you OK? Did you get the job at Bingham's? Has something happened? Have you had breakfast?'

Tad grinned, suddenly feeling pounds lighter than he had moments before. 'Not much. OK. Yup. Yup. Yup and nope.'

Becky put her hands on her hips in feigned exasperation. 'Now how am I supposed to know what all that means?'

'I just answered your questions. It's up to you to remember that string of 'em you asked. I answered 'em in order.'

Still pretending exasperation belied by her dancing eyes she said, 'Oh, get in here and sit down. I'll fix you some breakfast.'

'I was sure hopin' you would. Everything OK with you?'

'Everything's fine with me. But you look like something's awfully wrong. What happened?'

Over two cups of coffee and a huge plate of bacon, eggs and biscuits he filled her in. He started with acknowledgment of who he really was. He explained why he was there, and why he and Bingham had thought to keep those facts to themselves for the time being. Then he brought her up to date on the events of the preceding day.

She listened intently. He was surprised and pleased to note that she refrained from interrupting until he had finished. Her voice was soft, filled with conflicting emotions when she spoke. 'So why have you decided to tell me all this?'

Tad took a deep breath, staring into the deep blue-green pools of her eyes, as if unable to tear his own eyes away from them. He swallowed hard, and took another deep breath. 'I . . . it's been botherin' me some that I wasn't totally honest with you the day we met. Well, that's not entirely true, either. The fact is, it's been botherin' me a whole lot, ever since. I wanted you to know who I really am, and why I'm here.'

He hesitated. He took a deep breath, then lunged into what he wanted most to say. His words poured out swiftly, as if afraid to hesitate, afraid that if he even slowed the flow of words the least bit, he would lose his courage. 'I'd really like to get to know you a whole lot better. I hope I ain't too forward sayin' this, but I ain't been able to get you out of my mind since we met.'

'Haven't.'

'What?'

'You haven't been able. Ain't isn't a word.'

'It ain't?'

'It isn't.'

'You sound like a school teacher.'

'I am a school teacher. And I have to get to work. School is due to start in about half an hour.'

'Does that mean you ain't gonna answer my question?'

'I haven't heard you ask a question.'

He searched her eyes, trying desperately to fathom whether she was being lighthearted but wanting him to continue, or just willing him to go away and leave her alone. 'I think I asked . . . well, what I'm wantin' to ask, is if it'd be OK if I got to know you better.'

She started to respond with some witty come-back, then thought better of it. Her eyes searched his intently before she answered. 'Is that why you wanted to tell me all this?'

He nodded. 'I ain't . . . sorry. I'm not sure why . . . well, yeah. I do know. I just couldn't ride on back to the ranch without stoppin' in to see you first. I want you to understand what's happened. I want you to know who I am. I want to know you won't hate me 'cause I had to kill some of the ones rustlin' Bingham's cattle.'

She looked away from him finally, clearly thinking hard. She returned her gaze to his. 'I am relieved, frankly. I probably shouldn't say this, because I don't want you to think me forward. I never was very good at pretending, though. I was very attracted to you when we met. I knew you weren't being completely honest. It was obvious that you are used to using a gun, and very confident of your ability. I was really afraid you were a hired gunman or someone on the run from the law. I have tried very hard not to think about you, for that reason. But I haven't been able to get you out of my mind either. I . . . well . . . yes, I'd like to get to know you better too. I really hope you'll spend as much time in town as you can.'

He fumbled in his mind for words, trying to refrain from a shout of exultation, wanting to sound suavely confident and sure of himself but feeling like a stammering young boy with his first crush on that girl he's afraid to even talk to. In the end, all he managed to do was stare at her like a love-stricken schoolboy and swallow noisily several times.

She rescued him from his dilemma. 'I really do have to run. Will you still be in town when school's out?'

He shook his head, trying to ignore the instant disappointment that dimmed her eyes. 'I gotta get out to the ranch and fill the boss in on what I found out in Churchville. But I'll get back to town the very first chance I get.'

'I'll be here,' she said simply.

As she moved past him to the door, she stopped. She stood on tiptoe and planted a quick kiss on his astonished lips. Then she was gone.

He stood there a long while, his finger lightly touching the spot where his lips still felt that magical touch. He suddenly wanted more than anything in the world to forget all about his job, the rustlers, the ranch, everything except one incredibly beautiful woman.

7

'I reckon you must be the slaughter house pair.'

Oz and Verle Dutcher looked at the half-circle of hard faces focused on them. Totally surprised by eight riders, they had ridden into a trap they should have spotted from a distance. They were only two. Two against eight is impossible odds. Two working cowboys against eight professional gunfighters, practiced killers, is far worse than impossible.

More than five miles from the ranch, the duo had no hope of receiving help from any quarter. They masked their unease as best they could. It was not at all convincing.

'What're you talkin' about?' Oz countered. 'And who are you boys? This here's Flyin' E Bar range, and you boys sure don't ride for us.'

'We ride where and when we choose,' the other man retorted. 'Are you the pair that cut down some of our friends in cold blood?'

'Don't know what you mean,' Oz lied.

'Like hell you don't,' the response came instantly. 'Arapaho tracked their horses back onto your land. He said they was all killed by two men that was holed up behind a bunch of cedars. The only way two men could've got the drop on that bunch is if you opened up without even givin' 'em a chance.'

Oz quickly scanned the arc of hard eyes. He knew without any doubt that his life, and that of his companion, the hand everyone simply called 'Dutch,' was over. That being the case, there was no need to make any pretense. Any plea he might make would be futile. Any effort to avoid the inevitable would be, at best, ineffective. In keeping with the nature of hard men in a hard land, he decided he'd just as well enjoy what he could before he died.

There is something strangely freeing about knowing your life will be over within minutes. Nearly all the things normally fretted and fussed over become meaningless. Fear itself disappears. Normal caution, even, seems suddenly irrelevant, unnecessary. Despair of life often comes, in that instant, with a rush of irrational jubilation. So does the urge to get it over with as quickly as possible.

Responding to that rush of irrational jubilation and adrenalin, Oz grinned suddenly. 'You boys sure do over-rate yourselves somethin' awful. You ain't half as good as you think you are. We hollered at them friends o' yours. We told 'em to throw up their hands, seein' as how we caught 'em red-handed runnin' off pertneart a hundred head of our steers. They figgered nine to two was too good a odds to do that, so they started shootin' first. Like I said, you boys over-rate yourselves somethin' awful. Us two just had them nine fellas plumb outnumbered, outgunned an' outclassed. Matter o' fact, we got 'em outlived, too. Just in case you hadn't noticed that.'

'There ain't no way you coulda done that,' the speaker among the outlaws expostulated.

Oz's grin broadened. 'You didn't by chance check them boys' guns did you, to see how many holes they went and blowed in the air? Like I say, there was nine of 'em. They prob'ly got off fifty shots or more. Nine of 'em just wasn't nowheres near enough. By my count, there's only eight of you today. That's even worse, for you. Maybe you boys had best tuck your tails betwixt your legs and trot on off to home afore you find out how outgunned and outclassed you are.'

Several of the outlaws exchanged furtive glances, suddenly doubtful for the first time, puzzled by the grizzled foreman's bland confidence.

Their leader held no such hesitance. He glanced to both sides of himself, taking in the row of his cronies. 'Boys, I think we just heard a confession of cold-blooded murder. Let's us tie these two windbags up and see how loud they crow when they're dancin' on the end of a pair o' ropes.'

As if it were a signal, eight hands streaked to holstered weapons. Eight six-shooters leaped into well-practiced hands, spitting instant death within a fraction of a second.

As if attuned to the same signal, Oz and Dutch instantly dropped from their saddles, putting their horses between themselves and the deadly hail of lead focused on them. Even as they did, Oz's hat spun from his head, pierced by a .45 caliber bullet. The top of Dutch's left shoulder felt the sharp bite of a passing slug that didn't quite miss. More bullets whined and whizzed past their ears and over their heads. Long furrows appeared abruptly on the seats and across the cantles of both saddles.

Their own guns were in their hands just as swiftly. The first shot from each of their pistols swept an outlaw from his saddle.

At the same split-second, an unseen rifle barked. A third outlaw lurched from his horse, dead before he struck the ground.

The shot from a totally unexpected direction brought an eye-blink of hesitation to the would-be lynch mob. In that eye-blink, two more of their number left empty saddles on their way to perdition. A second shot from the unseen rifle emptied yet another saddle.

In less than three seconds the confrontation was over. Between two and three dozen shots had been fired. Six squandered lives were erased from the roster of the human race.

The remaining two reacted with incredible speed, borne of frightened desperation. Ducking low over their saddle horns, they whipped their horses around. Spurs dug fiercely into the sides of their mounts, propelling them to full speed in three jumps. Running flat out, the pair reined their horses first one way, then the other, in an evasive pattern of zigs and zags. They continued spurring frantically, urging their mounts to greater speed. With each stride their hope grew that they might survive. Even so, they were stunned. What had seemed a childishly easy opportunity to avenge their fallen compatriots had turned into what had suddenly seemed almost certain death. They were both equally convinced they had blundered into a well-laid trap. They were nearly half a mile away before they slowed their flight. Even then, they watched over their shoulders constantly. Their actions betrayed the extent to which they were thoroughly spooked. Whether by their failure or by the death of so many of their comrades was less than clear to them.

Back at the scene of the carnage, two equally spooked cowhands looked at each other.

'You OK, Dutch?'

'More or less,' Dutch complained. 'One of 'em took a hunk outa my shoulder.'

'Hit the bone?'

'Nope. Don't think so. Just plowed a furrow on the way by.'

'Gonna plant spuds in it?'

Dutch grinned in spite of the pain. 'Well, that'd save havin' to warsh it out.'

'You'd have to keep it watered, though.'

'Yeah, that's the problem. I don't like gettin' that close to water when I don't have to.'

'I sorta noticed that, ridin' downwind from you.'

'Who opened up from the trees?' Dutch stopped the exchange of banter.

'We're about to find out. Here he comes.'

'Well, whatd'ya know! It's that new guy! Tad!'

'Danged if it ain't,' Oz agreed. 'What's he doin' clear over here?'

'You send him somewhere else?'

'No, I didn't send 'im anywhere in particular today.'

'Then how'd he get clear over here?'

'You fellas OK?' Tad called as he approached.

'Yeah, thanks to you,' Oz replied. 'I 'spect we'd have gotten two or three of 'em afore they did us in, but we didn't have no real chance to see sunset till you opened up. That did surprise 'em some.'

'Surprised me too,' Dutch observed. 'But I was a whole lot happier about the surprise than they was.'

'What're you doin' over thisaway?' the foreman demanded.

'Just lookin' after a couple fellas that I thought might get themselves in a heap o' trouble,' Tad grinned.

'You figgered they'd be out here lookin' for us?'

Tad nodded. 'I figured there was a good chance of it, anyway. I heard this guy they called Burly send a right capable lookin' fella to backtrack the dead guys' horses. He'd know by now they was done in by just two guys. That means he's gotta find out who those two are and get rid of 'em, before his grip on the country starts slippin'. You two were comin' over here in the same general direction, so I figured you just might step in somethin' if you didn't watch where you walked real careful.'

'So you been followin' us all day.'

'Yup,' Tad admitted with a nod. 'Hope you don't mind. I thought my help'd be more effective if I wasn't seen with you, if it came to that.'

'Well, I can't argue with you,' Oz observed. 'It sure did come to that.'

'You know any of 'em?' Tad querried.

It was Dutch that responded first. 'That first one I cut loose on was Billy Blassengill. He's . . . well, he was . . . one o' Westler's deputies. I'm bettin' you'll find a badge in his pocket.'

'Who's Westler?'

'Clyde Westler. Town marshal over at Churchville. Tough customer. Keeps things in line for Bligh. Makes sure nobody complains about Bligh's grip on the town. Not that anybody in Churchville would be there if they weren't bought off by all the money he's brought to town.'

'Perfect setup for a nest o' rattle-snakes,' Tad observed.

'It is that for a fact,' Oz responded. 'Has been for a long time. Everybody in the country knows it's a hangout for hardcases and guys on the run. We just didn't figure out that it was that organized, or that that's where all the rustlin' was comin' from. We didn't figure guys on the run would mess up a good hideout by bein' too active that close to home.'

'Seems plumb obvious now,' Dutch almost apologized.

'Today sure did wipe away any doubts we might've had,' Oz agreed.

'How come they call the place 'Churchville'?' Tad asked abruptly. 'I've only been there the once, but I don't remember noticin' a church at all.'

Oz chuckled. 'It was called that even afore Bligh showed up,' he explained. 'Sorta somebody's sense o' humor. Caldwell City ain't much of a city, but it's got twice as many churches as any town that size oughta have. One oughta be enough for any town. But you're right. Churchville ain't got any. It started out bein' called Bartlettville. Then some travelin' preacher come to town. Matter o' fact, he was the only preacher that ever tried to start up a church there. Brave talker. Took on the 'dens of iniquity' head on. There was two of 'em in town then. 'Bout all he gained was gettin' run outa town. They tarred an' feathered him an' rode 'im outa town on a rail. Needless to say, he didn't make no effort to come back. So somebody thought it'd be real funny to call the town 'Churchville'. The name stuck.'

Dutch lost patience with the meandering conversation. He brought it back to pertinent matters with a rush. 'So what're we gonna do about that nest o' varmints?'

Total silence settled over the trio for a long moment. It was Oz who finally broke the stillness. 'Well, we ain't gonna be as lucky again as we been the past couple o' set-to's. There ain't no way we can brace 'em right there in Churchville. No tellin' how many of 'em there really are. More'n fifty, I'm guessin. And pertneart every one of 'em is bound to be faster'n a rattlesnake and a dead shot. They all been livin' by their guns a long while, most likely. We'd need a whole army to go after 'em there. If they was to come after us in force, I ain't sure we could even hold 'em off at the ranch. They just might do that, too, now.'

'They sure know what ranch we're from by now,' Dutch concurred. 'Them two that got away'll make sure o' that. They'll have me'n Oz tagged as the two that got the rest of 'em, too.'

'Do you know who those two that got away are?'

Both of the ranch-hands shook their heads, so Tad answered his own question. 'I'm pretty sure one of 'em was a young guy that calls himself Rusty McCleary. I had a face-off with him in town the day I first rode in.'

'He the one that's been tryin' to get

next to that good-lookin' schoolmarm?'

'He's the one. He sorta had her backed into a corner oughta sight of everyone. I stumbled onto 'em and broke up his party. He thought some about callin' my hand, but decided against it.'

'He's pretty good at knowin' when to cut an' run,' Dutch observed. 'Today makes twice he dodged a bullet that shoulda had his name on it.'

'That don't answer what we oughta do now,' Oz fretted.

Tad offered a suggestion. 'Why don't you send someone around to the rest of the ranches, as well as the small outfits and the homesteaders as well. Explain what we've found out. Tell 'em we know for certain who's behind the problems. Have 'em all meet someplace, and figure out a plan of action.'

Oz jumped on the idea instantly. 'That makes a whole bunch o' sense. That'll stop all the risk of settin' off a range war between the two sides of us. That'll bring a pretty good bunch o' manpower and weapons into the picture on our side, too. Our place is about as central as anywhere. We can call the meeting for . . . oh . . . say about Friday. We'll plan on feedin' 'em all dinner, then we can spend the afternoon gettin' together on a plan.'

They rode back toward the Flying E Bar, feeling like they were finally on the way to a solution. As seems normal with the human condition, simple solutions most often prove maddeningly elusive.

8

Large gatherings in sparsely settled country generate a festive air. Gatherings of men long opposed to one another generate an instinctively hostile air. Gatherings generated by fear and circumstances that seem out of control generate a volatile air of suspicion, anger and trepidation. At the same time, the loneliness that lingers always at the corners of settlers on the frontier irresistibly draws even the most suspicious and recalcitrant to any promise of community.

The gathering at the Flying E Bar ranch headquarters bore the signs of all those undercurrents. The tension in the air was palpable.

Homesteaders eyed ranchers obliquely, conversing with one another in quiet tones. Ranchers and cowhands eyed the homesteaders, in return, with scantily concealed disdain. Small ranchers returned the nervous surveillance of the sodbusters and ranchers equally, feeling caught in the middle of potential enemies, and dangerously outnumbered.

Temporary tables, laden with food, were set up in the yard. Almost as if in orchestrated divisions, each segment of the assemblage filled plates, then sought out some of 'their own' with whom to find seats on the ground and eat.

The day was cool and sunny. That and full stomachs slightly ameliorated the tensions in the air. When Ezra Bingham stepped up on a large tree stump, most were ready to at least listen to what he had to say.

He thanked them all for coming. He thanked them as well for the restraint they had shown in the previous months, preventing an all-out range war. Then he explained what had been learned of the identity of the perpetrators of the massive rustling and frequent, random robberies that had deeply touched all of their pocketbooks.

'Who is this hell-on-high-red-wheels hotshot you're talkin' about?' Frank Goodman, one of the homesteaders demanded.

Ezra hesitated visibly. 'I'd just as soon nobody knows his name or what he looks like just yet,' he apologized. 'The fewer people that know him by sight, the better his chances are of surviving until we have a chance to get this bunch dealt with.'

The strident hostility in the homesteader's voice raised a notch. 'You ain't gonna tell us who he is or what he looks like, but we're supposed to take all this just on his word?'

'His word, along with that of Oz Peterson, my foreman,' Ezra rejoined. 'And Verle Dutcher as well.'

'Did Oz and Dutch go with him tailin' them dead men?' Louie Free, a small rancher, asked.

'No. Just the hand I hired,' Ezra replied.

Goodman's strident voice jumped in again. 'Then we don't even have the word of anyone we know. We know a bunch was involved, 'cause Oz says so. We know him. But we don't know if they was followed to Churchville or someplace like the Pine Tree Ranch.'

Bud Forestall jumped to his feet instantly. 'Now just a minute! You got no right to accuse me or any of my hands of being involved in any of this! If you think I'm a rustler, you walk over here and say so, and we'll settle it real quick.'

Goodman raised both hands in front of him. The stridency level of his voice lowered noticeably. 'Now I didn't mean that, Bud. I ain't sayin' that atall. I'm just askin' how we know this fella followed him to where he says he did.'

Verle Dutcher entered the conversation in an attempt to counter the question. 'I'll give you one danged good reason. One of the guys I shot was one of Westler's deputies. He even had his badge in his pocket. There ain't no question but that he work for Bligh.'

'Used to work for Bligh,' a faceless voice observed.

Nobody responded to the attempt at levity. Instead, Oscar Peterson followed up with an observation of his own. 'Frank, those boys we sent to perdition was all laid out in Caldwell City by the undertaker for three days. Did you see any of 'em you recognized from any outfit in the valley?'

'I rode in just special to take a look at 'em,' a homesteader offered. 'I recognized two of 'em, from seein' 'em at that big fancy saloon in Churchville, all right.'

As if catching himself in a verbal slip, his eyes darted to his wife. She glared at him with sudden and undisguised fury. 'Understand,' he stammered, 'I just rode inta town over there for some supplies. I don't know who mighta been hangin' around inside the saloon. I just seen them two guys loungin' around on the street out front.'

A sudden air of breathlessness wrapped the potential domestic explosion in uncomfortable silence. Twice, Goodman started to offer more argument, but clearly could not think of any way to dispute what was being said. Uncharacteristically for his endlessly contentious nature, he shrugged his shoulders, folded his arms, and fell silent.

Bill Hardy, a young homesteader whose wife and two children had welcomed the opportunity to socialize, seized the opportunity to turn the conversation to a more constructive bent. 'So what are you suggestin' we do, Grunt?'

His use of the rancher's nickname had the effect of a loud expulsion of intestinal gas at a church social. Eyes darted from Hardy to Bingham and back. It was one thing for other ranchers, and even for cowboys, to use the term of friendly familiarity. It was quite another thing for a slightly arrogant young sodbuster to do the same.

Bingham, himself, seemed not to notice nor be offended. 'If we all stand together, we got a whole lot more men and guns than the whole outfit of

Bligh's. I'd say the best course of action would be to ride over there together and clean out that viper's nest.'

'You mean just go bustin' in there and kill 'em all?' an incredulous voice asked.

Bingham shook his head. 'If we show up with enough guys to have 'em out-manned and out-gunned, most of 'em will light out in a hurry. They didn't all live this long fightin' fair odds. They'll cave in quick, I'm thinkin'.'

'Bligh wouldn't,' Lars Nelson, an older homesteader disagreed. 'Him and that small army he calls his 'peacekeepers' would fight to the death to protect that little empire he's got over there — '

'He's bought up a lot of land around there, too,' Louie Free spoke up again. 'I heard he'd bought out several homesteaders, so I checked at the recorder's office. He's got title to a pretty big chunk of country over there.'

Lars continued as if Louie hadn't interrupted. ' — and if we go bustin' in there like the cavalry, how we gonna keep the decent people of Churchville from gettin' killed too?'

Goodman couldn't pass up the opportunity to offer an argument. 'If there were any decent people in Churchville, they'd have packed up and left a long time ago. The only people left there are the ones that like doin' business with gunslingers, outlaws and whores.'

A woman's voice lifted from the edge of the yard. 'Even Sodom and Gomorrah had one good family.'

The unexpected comment, and the greater surprise of the feminine voice injected into the discussion, silenced everyone for a long moment. It was Lars Nelson who broke the silence. 'I'd say we'd be well advised to send someone to Laramie. Talk to the US marshal there. Get the territorial government to do somethin' about it.'

'Either that or talk to the territorial governor himself, and have him send in the army,' another voice concurred.

'It sure ain't nothin' we got any business tryin' to do all by ourselves,' yet another chimed in. 'We ain't vigilantes.'

'Especially those of us that has womenfolk and kids,' another agreed.

'An all-out range war's the last thing we need,' yet another voice declared. 'Even if all of us is on one side, it'd be an all-out war for sure. I seen about all the war I wanta see in one lifetime.'

Lars spoke up again. 'How about sendin' that fella you hired to Laramie? He's the one what can answer the government's questions.'

Other ideas were tossed about for another hour. In the end, not much was decided. It was clear the bulk of the residents of the area were far from ready to band together as a militia. They were especially unwilling to commit to doing so under the command of a stranger.

From the vantage point of the barn's hay mow, Tad watched and listened. Little by little the conviction grew in him that there would be no help from anyone except the one ranch he worked for. It would, in other words, be mostly up to him to stop the rampant rustling and crime spree of Bligh's bunch. With that conviction, a parallel conviction began to grow that he would not survive to do so.

9

'Whatd'ya make o' that, Dutch?'

Verle Dutcher's lips were drawn into a thin line. 'Somebody's runnin' a long rope,' he gritted, 'that's for sure.'

They both studied the cow and calf much longer than necessary. Both had known the obvious conclusion at first glance. The cow bore the 777 brand of Arthur Blankenship's ranch. The calf was newly branded with a T-Slash-S brand.

Tad shook his head. 'I don't know. I can't believe anybody'd be dumb enough to dab his own brand on a calf that's still suckin'. That just makes it way too obvious to anybody.'

Dutch's tone was belligerent. 'Well, what else can you make of it?'

Tad hesitated before answering. He curled a leg around the pommel of his saddle as he watched the cow — calf pair. After several seconds he said, 'I hear that Blank bought a couple of them fancy white-faced bulls last year?'

'Yup. Four of 'em, actually, from what I heard. Paid a pretty penny for 'em, too.'

Tad continued, 'I wonder if maybe he's registered an extra brand or two, and he's using a different one on the calves sired by them high-priced bulls.'

'So he can tell how well they do?'

'Yeah, that and to keep from breedin' the heifers back to the same bull they came from, if he keeps 'em for breedin' stock.'

Dutch frowned. 'That'd get right hard to do. He'd hafta keep them heifers away off somewhere from the rest of his herds, to make sure the bulls didn't get to 'em.'

Tad nodded. 'It'd take a little extra herding, but it wouldn't be all that hard to do. He'd just have to separate the herds before he turns the bulls into 'em.'

Dutch was far from convinced. 'Well,

maybe. Wouldn't hurt to ask Blank, though. If one of his hands is runnin' a long rope, he'd sure wanta know about it anyway.'

Tad nodded toward a distant ridge. 'If I ain't mistaken, we won't have to do that. Ain't that Buster Lang an' Jack Murphy comin' down off that ridge?'

Dutch followed the direction of Tad's gaze. 'Might be. Rides like Buster anyway. Too far for me to be sure. You got better eyes than I got.'

They sat their horses, waiting the twenty minutes for the other pair to join them. When they had exchanged pleasantries and a typical stale range joke or two, Tad said, 'We were just noticin' that calf over there that's sportin' a different brand from his ma. You boys usin' a different brand on calves outa them blooded bulls or somethin'?'

Both hands turned in their saddles and looked where Tad indicated. They looked at each other, then back at Tad. It was Buster who spoke. 'Not that we know anything about.'

'Whose brand is the T-Slash-S?'

'Never seen it before.'

The four studied the cow and calf for long moments, as if they had rammed up against something they couldn't reason a way around. Finally Murphy said, 'If someone's runnin' a long rope, he's too dumb to pull it off. Or to live long. Slappin' an off brand on a calf that'll still be suckin' for another couple or three months don't make no sense. There ain't no way nobody's gonna notice that in that length o' time.'

'Does make it plumb suspicious,' Dutch agreed. 'That's just exactly what me'n Tad was sittin' here talkin' about when you boys topped that ridge.'

Buster said, 'We was wonderin' what was so fascinatin' over here. Thought maybe you'd ridden up on a couple porcupines matin', and couldn't quit watchin'.'

Dutch's forehead furrowed in sudden thought. He took the bait better than even Buster had hoped. 'I hadn't never thought about that. How do porcupines manage to mate?'

'Real careful,' Buster responded instantly. Dutch's face instantly turned bright red. The others laughed uproariously at his expense.

When the 'gotcha!' moment passed, Tad offered, 'I gotta ride to Laramie the day after tomorrow or so. I'll stop in while I'm there and find out who that brand's registered to. That might give us an idea of what's goin' on.'

'Whatcha goin' to Laramie for?' Jack querried.

'Talk to the US Marshal. See if we can get somethin' done, now that we know who's behind all the rustlin'.'

'Ain't gonna do you no good,' Buster asserted.

'Why's that?'

'Been tried afore. He lost a couple deputies, then he just plumb backed off. Ain't nobody been able to get him to even look this direction since.'

'That doesn't make a lot of sense,' Tad pondered. 'If he knows the

117

situation, and he's already lost a couple men, it seems like he'd be whippin' up here with a small army deputized to find out what's goin' on and who's behind it.'

'Ain't happened so far,' Jack observed.

'Ain't gonna, neither,' Dutch echoed. 'He's in somebody's pocket, sure's shootin'. Bligh's, most likely.'

'Well, I'll have a talk with him, when I go to Laramie,' Tad reiterated.

The pair of 777 riders shrugged their shoulders.

'You boys'll let Blank know about this?'

'Sure, we'll let 'im know. We'll even let 'im know you pointed it out to us, seein' as how it's your initials in that brand.'

Tad's eyes darted back to the calf in question. He felt the blood drain from his face. 'That hadn't even occurred to me,' he confessed. 'It sure is, though. Now that doesn't make any sense at all.'

'Might, when you find out whose brand it is,' Dutch opined.

'Well, that'll happen day after tomorrow, or right soon after that,' Tad responded.

They parted company. Tad failed to wave or acknowledge the pair's leaving, lost in thought about the implications of that brand. Little did he know the trip to Laramie would be longer than he anticipated in transpiring.

10

'He showed me a very official looking paper that said the brand was registered to you.'

Tad studied Rebecca's worried eyes. He was torn between being lost in their liquid depths and concern over the agitation they conveyed. 'Why would he have something like that?'

'He said he had ridden all the way to Laramie just to find out who owned that brand.'

'Since he doesn't work for any of the ranchers anyway, why would he care?'

'I asked him that. He gave me a whole speech about being concerned about the rampant rustling. He said the area needed law and order. He said he wanted to be a good citizen. It sounded like he'd memorized the whole speech. There were several words in it that sounded like he wasn't sure what they meant.'

'Real sanctimonious, though, huh?'

'He'd have made Reverend Fisher sound like a sinner.'

'Why did he show it to you?'

Her eyes searched his for a long moment, then lowered to the floor. When she raised them to meet his gaze again they were misty with emotion. 'I . . . guess I've said some things that have led people to believe . . . I mean . . . well, maybe something I've said made people think that you and I . . . that we . . . I mean — '

He interrupted her stammering effort to answer his question. 'You ain't, just by chance, given folks the idea you think I'm in love with you or something have you?'

Rebecca turned a brilliant shade of red. Her eyes searched his intently, trying to determine whether he was teasing or offended. When he failed to offer immediate reassurance, the red of her face faded to an unnatural pallor.

Tad stretched the strained silence

almost to the breaking point. When he thought he had pushed it as far as he dared, he continued as if his thought hadn't been interrupted. 'Because if you have, that'd make me just about the happiest man west of the Mississippi.'

It took almost two seconds before the import of his words soaked in. When their full import became apparent to her, color returned instantly to her face. Her eyes danced and filled with moisture, but she kept her expression teasingly irate.

'You monster!' she chided him. 'You deliberately made me think I had said something wrong, just to tease me! How could you?'

'It wasn't too hard,' Tad teased in return.

Her eyes turned suddenly serious. 'Will I scare you away if I tell you how much I've grown to love you, in just such a short time?'

'You couldn't scare me off with a shotgun,' he responded instantly. 'The only thing that'd ever get rid of me is for you to say you didn't love me. Then I 'spect I'd just crawl off in some corner and die.'

She moved up against him, putting both arms up around his neck, looking up into his eyes. 'Then tell me,' she invited.

'Tell you what?'

'Tell me you love me, you tormenting fool, before I stomp on your toe.'

'OK. I love you before you stomp on my toe.'

Careful not to overdo it, she instantly stomped on his toe. 'That's not what I mean and you know it.'

'OK. You stomped on my toe and I still love you. Satisfied now?'

Her eyes jumped and danced. 'You haven't even started satisfying me yet.'

'Well, we could get started, now that I'm here.'

'Not so fast, Romeo. Get the trouble taken care of and put a ring on this finger, then we'll work on that.'

Her mention of the trouble brought him back to unwelcome reality. He kissed her lingeringly, and felt her eager response ignite fire in him. Reluctantly he backed away. 'Speaking of the trouble, did McCleary say what he intended to do with that paper?'

She shook her head. Her eyes grew troubled. 'He just wanted to show it to me, and let me know in no uncertain terms that I'm wasting my affections on somebody that's either going to be run out of the country or hung as a rustler.'

'And, no doubt, offering himself as a consolation prize.'

'Something like that. He's been trying to get me interested in him since before you came to town.'

'I sorta noticed that the day I rode in. He hasn't tried pushing the issue, has he?'

She shook her head again. 'Not in any way except trying to convince me to choose him instead of you. Rusty has always been a perfect gentleman around me.'

'Except that day I rode in.'

'Well, yes. Except that day. And I

wasn't really afraid of him then. I think he was just teasing, more than anything. If I'd given him the kiss he wanted, he'd have probably been embarrassed to death.'

'I wouldn't count on that.'

'He's really been upset about us, I know that.'

'Then he knows how things are between us?'

Her face reddened again. 'Well, yes. I suppose so. I mean . . . well, face it. You're in love with a real blabber-mouth. I can't talk to anyone for five minutes without saying something about you. I'm sure it's obvious to everyone that knows me that I'm in love with you. I mean, even when I'm just talking to Tessie or someone, I constantly find myself saying something about — '

He couldn't resist the opportunity to pull her to himself again and smother the torrent of words with his own lips.

Disappointment flooded her eyes when he pulled away again. 'Is something wrong?'

'Too many things,' he responded. 'I gotta go. I gotta get back out to the ranch. There's some things I gotta do before I go to Laramie, then I gotta ride down there and see what I can get done with the law.'

The disappointment that had flooded her face filled her voice as well. 'Then I'm not going to see you for a while?'

'It'll be a few days, at least. I'll get back as quick as I can.'

'When are you going to Laramie?'

'Day after tomorrow, if I can get the other stuff done first.'

'You will be careful, won't you? I'd die if something happened to you.'

'So would I, most likely,' he countered.

She assumed a disgusted pose. 'That is not something to be taken lightly.'

'I don't 'spect I'd ever take a hunk of lead lightly. Lead's pretty heavy.'

She stamped a foot in exasperation. 'Tad Strong, I will not have you joking about the possibility of your getting killed. You have to take that seriously.'

'Oh, if I get killed, I'll take it plumb seriously.'

She started to stamp her foot again, then abruptly changed tactics. She grabbed him by the neck and pulled his face down to hers. She kissed him passionately, her tongue darting abruptly past his lips, teasing the tip of his tongue, then retreating. She pulled away. 'Just remember what you have to live for, and take care of yourself,' she admonished. Then she added, in a plaintive tone, 'for me?'

He traced the tips of his fingers downward along the side of her face. His voice was husky with a potent mixture of emotions. 'I will,' he said, and turned quickly away out the door.

He had the most difficult time of his life keeping his mind concentrated on the certain attempts at his life he knew were coming.

11

'They're sure due to be makin' another stab at them steers.'

Tad's raised eyebrows asked a silent question. When Bingham failed to acknowledge the unasked question, he turned to Oscar Peterson, the ranch foreman. 'Do you want me and Luther to check on 'em, Oz?'

Rather than answer immediately, Oz glanced at the ranch owner. 'You want just two of 'em goin', Grunt?'

Bingham scratched behind his left ear thoughtfully, skewing his hat crookedly on his head in the process. 'Well, three'd be better if you can spare 'em from what you had planned.'

Oz nodded. 'I can do that. Dutch, Luther, Tad, you three check 'em out. Try not to get into another all-out gun battle if you can manage. If they tryin' again to drive a bunch of 'em off, send one guy back for reinforcements. Lay low and tail 'em till the rest of us get there. Then we'll try to corral a few o' them sidewinders.'

All three knew what chances there would be of any such action. If they did discover the rustlers in action, by the time they sent for reinforcements and set up an attack, the cattle would be half way to wherever they were driving them.

They saddled their horses, packed what they thought they'd need into saddle bags and bedrolls, and rode out together. They were less than a quarter mile from the ranch, riding at a brisk trot, when Dutch sidled his horse close to Tad's. 'You really gonna wait for extra help if we catch 'em runnin' off steers again?'

The question struck Tad as uncomfortable. He was just a hired gunman, very transparently masquerading as a cowhand. The foreman had issued the orders. Even so, he knew every hand on the ranch, including both the owner and the foreman, looked to him for leadership.

'Depends on whether we think we can,' he admitted. 'I don't wanta get two of us killed because we sent the third man back for help.'

'Just what'd happen, too,' Dutch groused. 'Take away a third of our guns, an' hope we ain't both dead by the time Luther gets around to meanderin' back.'

'Who said I'd be the one ridin' for help?' Luther objected.

'Yeah, I might decide that'd be my job,' Tad offered.

'In a pig's ear!' Dutch expostulated. 'If you ride off from a showdown with them varmints I'm gonna be so close behind you my horse's nose'll be rubbin' your horse's tail.'

'Him an' me both,' Luther agreed. 'I'll stand with you against most anybody you've a mind to face, but I ain't takin' on Bligh's outfit without you.'

'Don't put too much stock in me,'

Tad argued. 'I put my britches on one leg at a time just like you boys.'

'Yeah, but once you got 'em pulled on, you shoot like half a dozen o' me,' Dutch declared. 'You're the first man I ever seen that could outshoot Oz, and Oz just pertneart don't miss. He still ain't stopped talkin' about your shootin' when you two tangled with Bligh's boys. He says you switched from one gun to the other so quick he thought a third guy had showed up to help.'

Talk dwindled away as the three studied the range for signs of moving cattle. They rode over the side of a deep gully, filled with brush in the bottom, and made their way toward the far side. Abruptly Tad whipped his rifle from the saddle scabbard. He lifted it to a shooting position in one, smooth, continuous motion, firing at almost the same instant the stock contacted his shoulder.

The other two jerked in surprise, instinctively grabbing for their guns.

Their eyes darted the direction Tad's rifle pointed just in time to see a mountain lion topple out of a tree and land, motionless, on the ground.

Luther swore. 'I never even seen that catamount!'

Dutch just grinned. 'You unlimbered that rifle faster'n I can draw and shoot my pistol. You ain't no end o' surprises.'

'We might want to ride down the bottom a ways before we climb up over the top,' Tad suggested. 'If some of Bligh's boys are wanderin' about, they might've heard the shot and be waitin' for someone to show up.'

Luther looked both ways along the brush-choked gully and scratched his head. 'Be awful tough ridin', bustin' through all that brush. Might be better if I shinny up to the top o' the ridge and have a good look around, to make sure nobody's waitin' on us.'

'That'll work,' Tad agreed.

He immediately hooked one leg around the saddle horn, giving clear indication that if that was Luther's preference, it would be Luther that crawled to the crest to look around.

Muttering almost under his breath in good-natured protest, Luther dismounted and began the climb to the top. As he neared the crest he crouched lower and lower, at the last laying his hat aside and crawling on hands and knees until he had a clear view of the surrounding country.

As he did so, Dutch querried, 'You gonna haul the catamount home?'

Tad shook his head. 'No point in it. It's almost impossible to get a horse to carry one. I had the gentlest horse I ever had go plumb nuts when I tried once.'

Dutch agreed, a rueful expression making his face almost comical. 'I know what you mean. I tried to load one on an old mule once. That critter took pertneart ten minutes to take a bite of oats. He pertneart killed me gettin' loose, then ran off fast enough to beat a good horse.'

Luther returned and stepped back

into his saddle. 'Nothin' movin' as far as I can see.'

They scrambled their horses up the side of the gully and continued onward. In less than fifteen minutes Dutch jerked to attention. He pointed. 'Dust in the air.'

The other two followed the point and nodded in agreement. 'Couple miles away yet,' Luther guessed. 'Movin' this way, though.'

'S'pose that's them?'

'I'd bet on it.'

'What way you reckon they'll come?'

'If they're stayin' to low ground, like they'd most likely be a-doin', they'll follow Watkin's Draw all the way to where they can ford the crick.'

'How far is that draw?' Tad asked.

'Only about a quarter mile ahead of us.'

'How narrow is it?'

'Fairly narrow some places. Why?'

Tad's eyes were bright with adrenalin and anticipation. 'The wind's straight toward where they'll be comin' from.

Let's drag that mountain lion over there and leave it in the narrow spot. When the steers get a whiff of it, they'll go plumb berserk. That'll keep the rustlers busy while we try to get the drop on 'em.'

The contagion of his excitement infected the others instantly. 'There's a perfect spot for it right straight ahead of us. And a ways downwind, about where them critters are gonna get real restless, there's ridges along both sides with lots o' rocks to lay out behind.'

'I'll get the cat,' Dutch volunteered.

He ran his horse back to the gully containing the dead cat. He returned in minutes. The cat was tied to the end of his lariat. Its other end was dallied to his saddle horn. His horse continually minced along, side-stepping, jerking first one way, then another, clearly terrified of the burden being drug along behind it.

'Betcha two bits that horse blows up afore he gets all the way there,' Luther grinned.

'Double or nothin'?' Tad taunted.

'Forget that!'

'Then I ain't bitin' on that one.'

The words were no more than out of his mouth when it happened. The big mare Dutch was riding ducked her head and began bucking furiously, still trying desperately to escape the terrifying scent of the mountain lion that pursued her, even in death.

At the first buck, Dutch released the dally of his lariat. The horse's bucking moved her farther and farther from the hated cougar, until he was finally able to regain his control over her.

Grinning, Luther rode over, dismounted, picked up the end of the discarded lariat, and remounted his own horse. He took a quick dally and nudged his own horse forward. As soon as the mountain lion began to move, his horse began to react exactly as Dutch's had done.

With great effort, Luther kept his horse under control until he had moved the cat into the desired position, directly in the center of the anticipated course of the driven steers.

Within minutes thereafter, all three were nestled down in the rocks. They had little time to spare. By the time they were in place, they could already hear the whoops and hollers of the rustlers, driving nearly one hundred and fifty steers. 'Gettin' greedier all the time,' Tad observed.

The point riders' horses began to react to the wind-borne scent first. At almost the same time, their ears went back, lying flat against their heads. They began to toss their heads, roll their eyes, and prance nervously.

The right point rider cursed and hit his horse between the ears with the heel of his hand. Tad's jaw tightened, instantly elevating his dislike of the rustler to near hatred level. 'No way to treat a horse,' he grumbled to himself.

That, and all the rest of their efforts, were futile in controlling the increasingly agitated horses. At the same time, the lead steers began showing the same signs of fear. Those in front abruptly whirled and started trying to barge between those following. Even as they did, others caught the scent of mountain lion on the breeze and became just as unmanageable.

Rustlers from back along the sides of the herd rushed forward to help with whatever problem the lead animals were encountering. As soon as they did, they began to have the same problem with their own mounts.

In less than two minutes, a routine, docile drive of a placid herd of steers turned into pandemonium.

Into that pandemonium, Tad's rifle barked. His carefully aimed slug barely creased the rump of the horse whose rider had clubbed it on top of the head. He squealed in pain and overwhelming terror, plunging back the way he had come. Mindless of bit, reins or rider, he began to run as fast as fear could impel him.

That was all it took to inspire complete panic in the other rustlers' mounts as well as the cattle. In seconds they were all scattering across the range in a broad fan from the point of contact with the smell of their most feared predator.

Some of the horses paused to buck occasionally, before resuming uncontrolled flight. Others simply ran, flat out, bellies to the ground, for more than a mile before their riders could slow and calm them. Before that time, half the rustlers were picking themselves up from the ground, swearing furiously and favoring a variety of injuries.

Laughing as if watching a vaudeville show, Dutch asked, 'Should we go after 'em?'

Tad shook his head. 'We'd be right out in the open if we did. There's too many of 'em.'

'They ain't likely to try to gather the herd together again today anyway,' Luther concurred.

Dutch nodded in agreement. 'It'll take 'em most of the afternoon to catch up everybody's horses and get 'em settled down enough to ride.'

'You 'spect they heard you shoot?' Luther wondered aloud.

Tad shrugged. 'Maybe. Maybe not, with all that goin' on at the same time.'

'That was some piece o' shootin',' Dutch admired. 'Creasin' his horse thataway just when he was plumb panicked anyway.'

'When he gets home he'll see that crease and know what happened anyway,' Tad observed.

Both of the others considered it, then nodded their agreement. 'One or two of 'em will probably ride back here to find out what spooked everything so bad,' Dutch guessed.

'They'll figure it out in a hurry,' Luther replied.

'That ain't all bad,' Tad opined. 'That'll keep 'em lookin' over their shoulders for a while.'

'I'm bettin' they'll be back tomorrow to try again,' Dutch said.

'Maybe,' Tad considered. 'I'll ride

over along here tomorrow to check, but I doubt if they'll try again that quick.'

He would remember that statement with a good deal of regret.

12

So far, it appeared his fears were groundless. He had seen no trace of the rustlers. He would have bet his eye teeth they would return today, loaded for bear, intent on regrouping and driving off the herd they had abandoned in such disarray the day before.

Maybe, he thought fleetingly, they had decided to raid elsewhere. Maybe they had found easier prey. Maybe other, less-guarded cattle would be more appealing. Maybe skunks wouldn't stink any more.

He left a thick stand of timber, eyes darting everywhere for signs of horsemen. The range seemed devoid of human life other than his own.

The ground ahead swelled gently toward the top of a large hill. Tall grass swayed gently in the breeze. An eagle, wings spread regally, floated motion-lessly on an updraft. Tad relaxed more than he had allowed himself to do for many days. He breathed deeply the high, clear air.

He was more than half way between the timber and the crest of the hill. He would get no farther. A flash of motion to his left jerked his head around. First a hat, then another, then half a dozen heads appeared, moving fast, directly toward him. In that first stunned second, the heads of their horses emerged above the hill's crest, ears laid back, bits loose, running flat out.

He whipped his head back the other way, confirming instantly that a solid line of assailants were bearing down on him in a wide arc, all pouring over the top of the hill in fierce and concerted attack.

He spun his horse around. He clamped spurs hard into the animal's sides. He bent low over the gelding's neck. He yelled into the mount's ear.

The horse responded, leaping for-ward as if pursued by the devil himself.

In four strides he was running at top speed. The ground beneath turned to a greenish-brown blur. The front brim of Tad's hat blew up tight against the crown. The haven of timber looked impossibly distant.

Behind him, his pursuers rode in total silence. Nobody wasted breath yelling. Only the thunder of the horses' hoofs, muted by the tall grass to a husky rumble, gave voice to the grim purpose of the hunters and the desperate flight of the hunted.

Tad twisted enough to glance behind. There were at least two dozen men in pursuit, spread out in a wide arc. The swift glance was adequate to know they were mounted on horses as fast as, or faster than, his own.

He tried to convey his desperation to his mount, shouting in his ear, urging him to greater speed. The gelding responded, giving his utmost, straining every muscle, neck stretched forward, ears laid flat, nose flaring, mane and tail streaming behind.

They were less than a hundred yards from the timber when the first shots were fired. Tad wasted no concern on them. They were gaining, but they were still too distant. Only an impossibly lucky shot could threaten him yet.

He entered the timber at a dead run. He gave the gelding his head, lying flat on the animal's neck until the saddle horn pressed hard into his stomach. He watched ahead as best he could, hoping against hope he wouldn't get swept off by a low branch.

His right leg scraped hard across the trunk of a tree, ripping off small, low branches. He mentally gave thanks for good boots and heavy chaps, knowing his leg would have been ripped open to the bone without them.

Then they were abruptly out of the trees again. The land ahead lay open and flat for three hundred yards. He reined the horse slightly to the left, heading for a copse of aspens. He was nearly to it when the first of his pursuers broke out of the timber behind him. They began firing again immediately. Still too distant for anything accurate, they nonetheless kicked up dirt too close for comfort.

He reached the aspen grove and reined around the left end of it. Instead of entering the trees, he angled toward another distant stand of pine and spruce, using the aspen copse to shield him from his pursuers as long as possible.

He was half way to the evergreen timber when his nemeses rounded the aspen thicket. They were grouped closer now, with the faster horses out in front, clearly gaining on him. They opened fire at once. Bullets buzzed angrily past his ears. Whipping past, they kicked up puffs of dirt on all sides. An occasional slug ricocheted from a rock and whined off into the distance.

He topped a gentle rise and dropped out of their sight into a shallow swale that angled at almost right angles to the direction of his flight. He reined his horse sharply left, taking advantage of its cover as long as possible. When he knew his pursuers must be nearly to the rim of that swale, he reined back right and up the other side.

The maneuver gained him a few precious yards of lead, putting his hunters again at the outer limit of their rifles' range. He headed toward the timber, urging his mount to its utmost effort.

He was just entering the timber when he felt the animal falter. He instinctively kicked free of the stirrups as the gelding went down. The worst had happened. A chance shot at the limit of its range had found the gallant animal and brought it down.

Tad rolled free and came to his feet instantly. He leaped back to the horse and jerked his rifle from the saddle scabbard. Taking cover behind a tree at the edge of the timber, he fired five quick shots at the horsemen seeking his death. Three men dropped from suddenly empty saddles. A fourth thrown clear when his horse went down. The rest hauled their mounts to a stiff-legged stop, leapt from their saddles, and began a withering return fire, directed at their adversary.

Their bullets found no mark. Before the echoes of his fifth shot had faded, Tad had wheeled, running at top speed back through the timber. He emerged suddenly into the open again. There was nothing in front of him but open range.

He knew he could hold out only for a time in the timber, with no hope of victory over so many. Every man in that party would be a crack shot, intent on his death, knowing if they returned with another report of failure Bligh would kill them in a fit of rage.

He set out on a dead run, putting as much distance between them and himself as he possibly could before they realized there was no return fire coming from the trees. He was barely two hundred yards into the open when he heard the shooting slow and stop. He was three hundred yards away when he heard the horses crashing through the brush and low branches.

Then he topped a low rise, escaping momentarily their line of vision. Breathing hard, he ran as fast as he could, praying for some miracle, knowing nothing less would allow him to live out the hour.

His path carried him up a gentle slope, bringing him into clear view of his would-be killers. A shout went up instantly. They knew with certainty he could not outrun their horses. There was no place for him to hide. He was dead if he continued to run. He was dead if he turned to fight. It was all but over. They had only to finish him at their leisure.

Tad ran desperately, hopelessly, determined to stay at the limit of their range as long as possible, then to make a stand of it. He knew he would die. The most he could hope for now was to take as many with him as possible.

His breath came in great gasps that burned in his throat like fire. The rifle in his hand seemed intolerably heavy. A red haze began to blur the horizons of his vision. A steady pattern of rifle fire stabbed at him, kicking up dirt. Bullets ricocheted off rocks, singing their wail of death into the distance.

Abruptly and unexpectedly, the ground dropped away beneath him. He jerked to a halt, teetering on the brink of a cliff. Bullets whining in the air around him; he leaned forward. At least a hundred feet below, a large stream made its way briskly along the foot of the cliff. It looked like it might be deep. If he jumped outward far enough, he might be able to avoid the jutting rocks and brush, and make it to the water. But from that height, would hitting even water kill him instantly? It was certain death to hesitate. It was almost certain death to leap.

He looked around desperately. He scrambled over the edge, escaping for a moment the hail of searching, angry, deadly leaden projectiles. At his feet was a large rock, weighing perhaps fifty pounds. He raised his head, noting the closeness of his pursuers.

Acting on impulse, he hefted the large rock. He watched through the grass at the cliff's edge as his pursuers leaped from their horses and ran forward, rifles at the ready.

He turned and heaved the rock as far outward as he could. Instantly he dove to his left, lying flat, crowding back into brush that grew below a lip of ground that jutted out slightly from the face of the cliff.

He heard the rock hit a rock once on its downward flight. Just after he heard the sound, he felt, rather than saw, several men rush to the edge of the cliff.

'There!' one of them yelled.

Just as he did, Tad heard the rock hit the water below with a mighty splash.

'He jumped,' another voice shouted.
'I seen him hit the water.'
'Don't matter. The fall'll kill 'im.'
'Maybe not.'
'Everybody! Fan out downstream.

Cover that crick for a hundred yards. If he comes up, fill 'im full of lead.'

Booted feet hastened to obey. Crowding back into the brush, trying to be invisible, Tad could see the ends of half a dozen rifle barrels thrust out past the top of the cliff.

Nothing moved. Nobody spoke. A mosquito buzzed in Tad's ear, then landed and began to seek a meal of warm blood. He resisted the almost intolerable urge to move, to shake his head, to swat the pesky insect away.

'He ain't comin' up.'

'He couldn't stay under this long without drownin'.'

'I told you it'd kill 'im to hit water from this high up.'

'Saved us havin' to shoot 'im.'

'That's what I was lookin' forward to.'

'Yeah. Me too.'

'Let's go.'

'Watch a little longer. He might be hidin' down there, under the bank, playin' possum.'

'If he survived hittin' the water he wouldn't have enough left to play nothin'.'

'Let's go tell Bligh we got the SOB.'

'I'm pretty sure I hit 'im once.'

'I think I did too, just as he jumped.'

'I didn't even see 'im jump.'

'I just got a glimpse of 'im hittin' the water.'

The talk grew softer and more distant as they returned to their horses, mounted, and rode back the way they had come. Tad stayed where he was for half an hour, making sure no skeptical hand of Bligh's had lingered to wait for his body to float in the stream below. When he was certain nobody remained, he began to move his cramped muscles and stiffened joints.

Peering cautiously over the rim of the cliff, Tad took plenty of time to make sure no one remained of the band of men sent to kill him. When he was satisfied it was safe, he climbed back onto flatter land and began a very long walk back to the Flying E Bar.

13

'They didn't waste any time, did they?'

Oz Peterson and Ezra Bingham scowled at Luther as if it were he who had stolen a hundred and fifty head of prime steers. 'They was herdin' 'em back together afore Strong even made it back to the ranch, it looked to me like,' he reported.

'Figgered with him outa the way, thar warn't nobody gonna stop 'em,' Oz opined.

Luther glanced across the ranch yard. He grinned abruptly. 'Now there's one stove up fella,' he declared.

The other two turned to watch Tad's painful progress across the yard. Seeing the hand reporting to the foreman and owner, he obviously wanted whatever news Luther could afford. Getting there was another matter entirely.

Cowboys never walk unless it's

necessary. From the house to the barn, any self-respecting cowboy would mount his horse and ride across the yard. Tad was no different, even if he had spent more time than he wanted in towns, enforcing the law.

But he had run. He had run a long way. That unaccustomed run, fleeing for his life, would have left him stiff and sore for days. When that was combined with an eleven- or twelve-mile walk in riding boots, it was beyond severe.

'He walks like a ninety-year-old geezer,' Luther chortled.

'Try walkin' that far in a pair o' boots and see how well you walk,' Oz countered.

'I knowed a man once that kept a pair o' moccasins in his saddle bag just in case he had to do that,' Bingham observed.

'I think I'd just build a fire and wait for someone to come along,' Luther grinned.

'Somebody'd come along all right,' Oz countered. 'The same guys that was hell-bent on killin' 'im, that's who'da come along.'

'What's up?' Tad asked, approaching painfully.

'We was just gathered together here to admire how well you walk,' Luther teased.

'Just wait till tomorrow,' Bingham counseled. 'It's always worse the second day.'

'If it's any worse, you boys are gonna have to help me outa bed,' Tad declared.

Immediately he turned the conversation more serious. 'What's goin' on?'

Luther repeated his story. 'They came back an' rounded up them same steers. Run 'em off this mornin' already.'

'That's not surprising,' Tad observed. 'Might be the chance we're waiting for.'

Bingham frowned. 'Whatd'ya mean?'

'That's too big a bunch of cattle to just disappear. They'll be plumb easy to track. I'll follow 'em and find out what's happening to the stuff they steal.

They gotta be takin' it all somewhere.'

'You think you're in any shape to do that?'

'I'll be fine,' Tad protested. 'I'm a little stiff and sore, but I'll ride it off soon enough.'

'Better take a couple o' the boys with you,' Oz suggested.

Tad shook his head. 'They think I'm dead. If they're watching the place, and see a couple others disappear, they might get suspicious. I'll ride careful, stay out of sight, and we'll just let 'em think I'm dead for a while.'

Bingham nodded his agreement. 'I'll send a couple of the boys with an extra horse to retrieve your saddle and stuff.'

'There shouldn't be any need to tie anyone else up doin' that. They've already run your stock off. They'll be too busy gettin' back to Churchville so they can spend all the money they get out of 'em.' Tad said. 'I can lead an extra horse, get my saddle and gear, then turn the horse I'm ridin' loose. He'll come home. Then I can ride on from there and pick up the trail.'

'Are you sure you don't want anyone backin' you?'

'No need,' Tad assured him.

The first five miles were the longest Tad had ever ridden. It felt good to be off of his feet, but that's the only thing that felt good. Slowly, though, most of the stiffness began to wear away. By the time he reached his dead horse, he was feeling almost normal. Until he stepped out of the saddle.

That's when everything fell apart.

When his boots hit the ground, pain shot through his legs, his buttocks, his back. His knees buckled. He toppled sideways, grabbing for the trunk of a small tree to keep himself upright. He almost reached it. Instead, he fell heavily.

The horse he had ridden there grunted, faltered, then crumpled to the ground. As it hit the ground, the report of a rifle reached Tad's ears. Some part of his mind recognized that only his fall had dropped him from a hidden rifleman's sights, causing his horse to take the bullet intended for him.

The horse fell the wrong direction. It landed solidly atop the scabbard holding his rifle. He was left with only his .44 to defend himself against a hidden sniper with a rifle.

The words ran, unbidden, through his mind. 'Survived the trap by the cliff just to die here instead.'

Tad squirmed behind the trunk of the largest tree he was close to. He cursed himself silently. He had been certain the rustlers believed him dead. He had been certain they would leave nobody watching his dead mount for his return. Maybe they weren't. Maybe they were laying for whomever came looking for him when he failed to return.

They certainly knew he was alive now, though. Whoever was lying in wait would have set up closely enough to be certain of the identity of his target. He, at least, would know Tad had not leaped to his death from that cliff.

No second shot had followed the round that killed his mount. The shooter had to know it was the horse he had hit, not the man. Therefore, he was simply waiting until Tad moved, to pinpoint his position.

Tad studied the fallen animal. He could see the bullet hole in the stirrup leather. He knew what position the horse had been in. From that, he knew at least the direction of his would-be killer. He also knew that hidden gunman was even now watching across the sights of his rifle to determine his own location.

He began to inch his way slowly backward, keeping the tree between himself and that presumed spot. Pain shot through his legs and back with every movement. When he had more of the timber between himself and his enemy, he stood slowly, gripping the trunk of a small tree for balance and support. He gritted his teeth, clamping his jaw against the pain.

He stood still for several seconds.

Still holding to nearby trees, he began to walk in slow, painful steps.

As he began to walk, circulation and function began to return to his lower limbs. In a few steps he was able to begin walking almost normally, though each step still shot pain through his entire lower body. Steeling himself against it, he slowly, silently, worked his way through the timber at right angles from his assailant.

When he thought he was sufficiently far, he started creeping forward, watching for the edge of the neck of timber that concealed him. When he saw it in front of him, he went prone again, squirming his way slowly and silently to its edge.

From where he now lay, he could see the lay of the land clearly. There was no sign of movement, but he knew the sniper was out there, watching, waiting. He just didn't know exactly where.

Calculating again the direction from which the shot had to have originated, he guessed at a range of about a hundred yards, and began to look for anything that might conceal a gunman, and still give him a clear field of fire.

He could see only one place meeting the criteria. A pair of rocks were screened by low sage that had grown up in their shelter. The gunman almost had to be behind those rocks.

He scanned the area behind and to both sides of the spot. It appeared that less than a hundred feet behind the spot, a rise of ground hid whatever lay behind for a considerable ways. If he could back out of his current location, circle around silently, he just might be able to get behind his hidden adversary.

He immediately began working his way cautiously, silently backward. When he knew there was enough timber between himself and the other to screen him, he repeated the process of getting to his feet. He waited out the initial pain of standing, then loosened up protesting muscles adequately to allow him to walk.

He began to walk through the

timber, in almost a straight line from his original position. He was soon rewarded by feeling the ground dropping lower. He watched through the trees, guessing when he had passed low enough to screen him from the concealed gunman. Then he walked to the edge of the timber and looked out cautiously from behind a large tree.

He could see only a dozen yards in the direction of the sniper's position. To his right the ground fell away steadily, climbing back upward three hundred yards farther on.

He left the shelter of the trees, walking as swiftly as his loosening muscles allowed. He watched intently in the direction that he had fixed in his mind as the location of his assailant. He walked a wide circle, staying always well below the crest of the hill. When he was certain he was behind him, he walked forward, up the hill that screened him.

He stopped abruptly, almost toppling over from the different strain jerking to a halt put on those still stiff and uncooperative legs. A saddled horse was tied to a low bush less than twenty yards in front of him.

He held perfectly still as the horse eyed him, hoping against hope the animal wouldn't spook or snort. If it betrayed his presence, he had a problem.

For the first time since he had stepped from his own saddle, something went right. The animal watched him alertly, but made no sound.

Returning his attention to the threat at hand, he walked up the hill until he suspected he was about to come into sight of the other. Then he removed his hat and laid it on the ground. He dropped to hands and knees and crawled forward, slowly, silently, fearfully.

He had crawled only a few yards when he saw a slightest hint of motion. The smallest movement, visible only for a fraction of a second, he was sure was the tip of a hat's crown. He froze in place, not daring to breath. Gathering his feet beneath him, he rose slowly. Once again he felt the stiffness and lack of balance momentarily as he stood. It passed more quickly this time, leaving him standing erect, confident of his ability to move.

From his standing position he could clearly see the sniper, stretched out full length on the ground, watching over the sights of his rifle the spot in the timber at which Tad had disappeared. 'Patient killer,' Tad thought.

He stepped forward, slowly, silently. He slid his .44 soundlessly from its holster. When he was less than fifty feet from the would-be killer, he said, 'Lookin' for me?'

The reaction was instantaneous and swift. As if Tad's voice were the keeper on a spring-loaded trap, the prone man sprang into action. He whirled around, rolling over on the ground, whipping his rifle around to bear on Tad.

He was fast. Incredibly fast. If Tad hadn't already had his own gun in his hand, he might have been fast enough.

Tad's .44 roared before the man was entirely turned. It roared again, even as the man grunted and tried to continue his motion. It roared yet a third time as the gunman's finger tightened convulsively on the rifle's trigger, sending a bullet harmlessly into the Wyoming air.

He was dead even as his body continued the spin, throwing him onto his back. His arm, bereft now of the rifle it had held, continued the motion. It flopped onto the ground at a right angle to the body it had failed its last opportunity to serve.

Tad watched the dead gunman long enough to ensure himself the man was, in fact, dead. Then he walked back down the hill, mounted the other's horse, and rode him back to where his own dead mount, and the extra horse he had led there, awaited.

14

'Right nice bunch o' steers.'

The paunchy, middle-aged man turned from where he had been leaning on the top rail of the corral. 'Best I've seen this year,' he agreed.

Tad nodded toward the corralled herd. 'Your stock?'

'Yup. Bought 'em yesterday. Paid top dollar for 'em too.'

'Not near what you'll get when you ship 'em back east, though, I 'spect.'

The man eyed Tad carefully. 'That's why I'm in business. I'm a cattle buyer. I make a good living being the go-between for ranchers and packing houses.'

'Buy quite a lot of 'em here?'

'Most of my business is right out of here, as a matter of fact.'

'Hobb's Center seems an unlikely spot for that regular a supply of cattle.'

The man's eyes grew more cautious still. 'I would imagine part of that is my reputation for honest dealing and fair prices. A lot of ranches in this part of Wyoming drive their steers here just because they know I'll buy them.'

'You buy a lot of different brands, then?'

'Sure. Flying E Bar, like these, quite a bit. Always fine stock. I buy a lot of Triple Seven stock, H Bar H, Pine Tree, Double O, Mill Iron, you name it.'

'You know the owners of all them ranches, do you?'

The man began to glance around nervously. 'You sure ask a lot of questions. Who are you?'

'A man that asks a lot of questions,' Tad replied. 'I asked if you know the ranchers from all those brands you buy.'

'I don't have to know the owners personally. Their foremen, or whomever they choose to send in charge of a herd to sell, is just as good.'

'What if it's somebody that they didn't send?'

168

'What are you saying?'

Instead of answering, Tad fired another question. 'Do you have a bill of sale on these steers?'

'Of course I do.'

'Mind if I see it?'

The man looked for a while as if he would refuse. The look on Tad's face changed his mind. He fished in the inside pocket of his vest and pulled out a piece of paper. He handed it defiantly to Tad.

Tad unfolded it and read the scrawled words: 'Sold to Hiram McCrowdey 153 head of steers, branded Flying E Bar. Jasper Smith.'

'You're McCrowdey?'

'I am.'

'Jasper Smith,' Tad read aloud. 'Don't know the name. Do you buy from him often?'

McCrowdey hesitated before answering, increasingly uncomfortable. 'A fair amount of the time. He's a field buyer. Buys directly from the ranchers, then sells to me.'

'Always has a bill of sale from the owner, I'm sure.'

'Of course. I wouldn't buy otherwise.'

'Have you ever checked those bills of sale to make sure it was the owner's signature?'

'Now why would I have to do that?'

'Might cost you a lot of money if you didn't.'

'How could it do that?'

'Well, just like that hundred and fifty-three head of prime steers right there behind you. I'm sure you paid a pretty good bit for them.'

'More than a pretty good bit.'

'And it's all lost. Gone like a snort in the wind.'

McCrowdey's face reddened abruptly. 'What are you talkin' about?'

'I'm talking about a hundred and fifty-three steers that were stolen from the Flying E Bar by rustlers. I work for the Flying E Bar. I was sent to track them, and find out what happened to them. I found them. I'm claiming them in the name of the Flying E Bar as stolen cattle. Now you have to turn them over to me and admit you made a very expensive mistake. Either that or claim they're your cattle, which you can't. That'd either make you a rustler, or in cahoots with the rustlers. Either one, if I'm not mistaken, is a hanging offense.'

McCrowdey's face drained of color. Sweat popped out across his forehead. 'Now listen here, I've got a bill of sale for those steers, perfectly legal and legitimate.'

'Perfectly phony and you know it. Let's you and me take a little walk over to the town marshal's office and see what he's got to say about it.'

McCrowdey's eyes darted about wildly, as if searching for some avenue of escape. Then, without warning, his hand emerged from the front of his vest holding a derringer. As if it had leaped there of its own accord, Tad's .44 roared an instant ahead of the bark of the small-caliber weapon. The force of the slug knocked McCrowdey backward enough that the bullet from his derringer nearly missed Tad. It burned along the side of his neck, leaving a raw furrow barely more than skin deep.

The sudden pain triggered further reaction. He instinctively fired two more quick slugs into the cattle buyer, impelling him backward against the rails of the corral. The derringer slid from his hand. He slid slowly down the fence, stopping in a sitting position, his head slumped forward.

Tad watched him for a brief moment, assuring himself the man was no longer a threat. He replaced the spent cartridges in his revolver with fresh loads from his belt. He holstered the weapon, then felt gingerly at the groove in the side of his neck.

Satisfied it was a superficial wound, he moved his neckerchief sufficiently to serve as a loose bandage. He turned and walked toward town and the marshal's office.

At the latter's office, he met with an

almost insolent unconcern. The town marshal was as paunchy as McCrowdey, but far less particular about his person. Tobacco juice stains colored the moustache that sagged well below the ends of his mouth. Stains of the same color formed a random pattern on the front of the vest that stretched across his ample stomach. 'You're lucky,' he informed Tad. 'McCrowdey's put several fellas away with that derringer of his. Right handy with it. Always self-defense, o' course, so's I couldn't do nothin' about it.'

'I don't suppose you could do anything about his buying stock he knew was stolen either,' Tad challenged.

The jab failed to ruffle the marshal in the least. 'He always had a bill o' sale. That's all the law says I'm s'posed to check. I ain't got no way to check signatures, to make sure who's it is.'

Tad thought of several retorts, then decided it was a waste of breath. 'Well, I'll expect you to see that those steers are kept well fed and watered until I can send a crew to drive them home, since you weren't vigilant enough in your duties to keep your town from becoming a haven for stolen cattle.'

'Now see here,' the marshal blustered, 'That ain't my responsibility.'

'It is now,' Tad retorted. 'I just made it yours. And if it isn't done properly, you'll answer to me. Is that clear?'

The marshal clearly wanted to defy the demand. He just as clearly understood that it would be foolish in the extreme to do so. 'I'll see what I can do,' he said finally.

'Just see that you do,' Tad responded, emphasizing the word 'that.' He turned and walked out, not waiting for any further response from the would-be lawman.

15

It was anything but a joyride. Pain shot through his legs and back every time he shifted his weight in the saddle, every time he stood in the stirrups to restore circulation.

Another attempt had been made on his life. He had lost yet another horse to a rustler's bullet. The ride from there to Hobb's Center had been miserable. After his confrontation there with the cattle buyer, then that poor excuse of a town marshal, his mood was even worse.

The ride had been long, hot, windy, dusty, and almost every other form of uncomfortable that the treeless, rolling prairie of eastern Wyoming Territory could afford in summer. The wind, especially, wore away at Tad's mood as if directly abrading it with a constant scouring of fine sand. It chafed his face raw. It tugged ceaselessly at his hat. It filled his mouth and nose with dust. It made even his eyelids feel grainy and abrasive every time he blinked away the irritating bits of dirt.

It had blown that way all the way to Hobb's Center, where the railroad had its holding corrals for outbound cattle. It had blown just as badly all the way to Laramie. He wondered for the hundredth time how the wind could never cease, never rest, never calm in that part of the Territory.

In addition, the wind's constant tugging at his neckerchief kept the fresh wound on his neck raw and sore. It added measurably to the choler of his already dark mood.

At the end of that irritating ride was a nearly sleepless night. He tossed and turned in a sagging bed in a cheap hotel, where he could hear the sounds from at least half a dozen rooms. Some of those sounds made all too obvious the activity surrounding him. It drove home his own loneliness in ways he could not describe or understand. He had never minded living a lone life. Then he had met Rebecca, and his attitude suddenly changed. Now he felt the loneliness of his life in ways he had never experienced. That sense of loneliness only added to his disgruntled state.

He ate a greasy breakfast, that cost far too much, in the hotel dining room. He washed it down with too-weak coffee, then headed down the street to find the objective of his trip.

He hated Laramie, even in the best of times. He had lived in Cheyenne far longer than he was comfortable, and Laramie was worse. It teemed with people, fully half of them opportunists, hoping to influence territorial officials in one way or another. Most of them were burdened with an over-inflated idea of their own importance. They all seemed to be in a big hurry to get wherever they were going. It made the main thoroughfares a crowded, bustling maze to work his way through.

Like most westerners, Tad hated crowds of people to begin with. He also carried the typical westerner's deep-seated disdain for those with inflated egos. The combination served to sour his disposition even further, long before he got to the office he sought.

He found it, following the hotel clerk's directions, without incident. He shouldered his way through the door, already spoiling for a fight.

At least the man behind the modest desk met his entrance with an honest, steady gaze. 'Mornin',' he greeted Tad. 'How can I help you?'

'Stop all the danged rustlin',' Tad replied instantly, his voice both louder and harsher than he had intended.

The man showed neither alarm nor irritation at the abrupt answer to his question. In contrast, his eyes actually twinkled in response. A grin spread beneath a large moustache. 'Well that shouldn't be any real problem. Do you want me to take care of that in the whole territory this mornin', or should

I save part of it till tomorrow?'

The levity of the answer should have been the trigger that set off Tad's seething rage and frustration. For reasons he didn't understand, it had quite the opposite effect. The man's open good humor and ready wit served to defuse Tad's bottled-up frustration and pointless rage. He felt the tension drain out of him as if the man's words had pulled a plug from the bottom of his emotions. His expression, however, remained just as intense. 'Well, I figured the whole territory if you didn't have anything more pressin' this mornin'. You can do as you please with the rest of the day.'

'Well now, that's plumb generous of you,' the man replied. 'I'm glad you're not going to be unreasonable about it.'

He stood and thrust out a hand. 'I'm Heck Thurman. US Marshal for Wyoming Territory.'

'The heck you say,' Tad rejoined, taking the proffered hand, appreciating its firm, strong grip.

'Heck I do say. I have been called the other option a time or two. Along with several other things.'

'I can imagine. I haven't heard the name before.'

'It ain't too common. Do you think maybe my ma mighta had a hand in namin' me?'

'Might be. Prob'ly a good thing. Your pa likely didn't say 'oh, heck,' when he seen you.'

'That first look can be a shocker, all right. I got a deputy named Toad Benson. Imagine what it was like for his pa.'

Tad chuckled, at a loss for a rejoinder. The marshal steered the conversation. 'So who are you, and what can I do for you? You want a cup of coffee?'

'Well, sure, to the last question. The first one's gonna take a little longer.'

The marshal nodded and turned to the coffee pot sitting on the back edge of the stove that occupied the center of the room. He poured a steaming cup of the dark brew and handed it to Tad. Tad sipped it carefully, then nodded approvingly. 'Sure beats that left-over dishwater they serve at the hotel.'

'They do skimp on the beans some, I've noticed,' the marshal agreed. 'Where you from?'

'My name's Tad Strong. I ride for the Flying E Bar, up above Caldwell City.'

'Ah,' the marshal replied knowingly. 'I know both names, but not together. How long you been up there? You was a town marshal in Cheyenne a couple years, wasn't you?'

'Deputy,' Tad confirmed.

'How'd you end up clear up in Grand Valley?'

'Ezra Bingham looked me up in Cheyenne. Offered me a job findin' out who was stealin' him and the other ranchers blind. That sounded better than facin' every would-be gunfighter that wanted to make a name for himself in Cheyenne.'

'I'm not sure you improved your lot a whole bunch.'

Tad's expression reflected rueful agreement. 'You know the situation there, huh?'

'Better'n I'd like to,' Thurman admitted. 'I lost a couple good men up there, and didn't accomplish one danged thing.'

'I heard about that,' Tad acknowledged.

Some of Tad's irritation and frustration returned, and his voice took on a more accusing tone again, as he continued. 'But you didn't go back, or send anyone else.'

Thurman studied Tad for a long moment. When he spoke, it was not to respond to the implied question in Tad's statement. 'I'm guessin' you didn't ride clear down here to tell me what I already know.'

Tad took a long sip of the strong coffee. Then he started at the beginning, filling the marshal in on everything they had learned and done.

'You've cut a pretty wide swath through that valley in that length of time,' Thurman admired when he finished.

'Not wide enough. We haven't accomplished any more than your boys did, up to now. Except stay alive. And that just barely.'

'Well, yeah, you have,' Thurman argued. 'You cut down the odds quite a bunch, it sounds like. Maybe you put the fear o' God in a few of the others. Hard to tell. Most of all, you got some good solid information. Not enough, I'm afraid, though, to be able to go against my orders.'

Tad frowned. 'What do you mean, 'go against your orders?''

Thurman sighed heavily. 'That's something that's been stuck in my craw for over a year, but I can't do nothin' about it. I lost two good men up there. That ain't no big deal to the higher ups, but it sure is to me. I got orders from my superiors that I'm to . . . how'd they put it? I'm to 'stop wastin' good men chasin' something that's outa my league to begin with.' My orders are to ignore whatever's goin' on up there, trust my superiors to handle it, and tend to the rest of the territory.'

Tad was incredulous. 'Why in the world would they do that? That makes it sound like Bligh's got your superiors bought off.'

Thurman sipped his own coffee before he answered. 'Well,' he said finally, 'I got no proof of anything like that, so I couldn't say that. All I can say is that's what my orders are.'

'So you can't do anything?'

Thurman's eyes flashed momentarily. Almost at once the fire that briefly flashed was masked behind a look of tired resignation. Hard lines appeared at the corners of his mouth, below the tips of his moustache. 'As long as I'm a US marshal, I guess I got to go by my orders. I'll tell you what I can do, since they didn't specifically tell me I couldn't. I can contact the army, tell them everything you've told me, and ask them to send a unit down there to investigate. I'll suggest they maybe look you up for information and guidance. I can't do any more than that and still keep my job. At least doing that much might keep me able to look myself in the face when I shave of an evenin'.'

The statement triggered a totally unrelated response from Tad. 'You shave at night?'

Thurman laughed abruptly. 'Now don't that take the cake! Here we are talkin' about a nest of thieves and killers and rustlers, me with my hands tied tighter'n a calf about to get branded, and you wanta talk about what time o' day I shave. But yeah, as a matter of fact, I do shave at night.'

'How come?'

'Well, in the winter time, my face don't get near as cold as it does if I shave of a mornin'. And the plain fact is, the missus appreciates it. She's a whole bunch more receptive most times if I'm fresh shaved.'

Tad acted embarrassed to have asked. 'Sorry. None o' my business. So, you can't do a blessed thing to help us, is what you're saying?'

'No, that ain't what I'm sayin'. I'm sayin' I can't round up a posse and go ridin' up there lookin' to start a war. But the army danged well can, and I'll do my best to get 'em to look into it.'

'And how long is that going to take?'

Thurman looked uncomfortable. 'Well, you know the army. If it rattles a response from the Territorial Commander, they'll get right on it. If it doesn't, he'll send a report to Washington. Four or five copies, properly written. They'll discuss it from now till the middle o' next summer. Then, just maybe, they'll send a delegation from Washington to look into it.'

'If you were a gamblin' man, what kind of odds would you give either way?'

Thurman shook his head. 'I ain't, and I wouldn't.'

'So what you're really sayin' is that we're on our own. Every honest man in Grand Valley's been stolen blind for the past three years. They're all on the verge of goin' broke. A range war's a strong possibility. I been shot at, hunted, bushwhacked and beaten half to death, just to find out who's behind it. And you tell me the law can't help us.'

If there had been a knot hole in the rough floor of his office, Heck Thurman looked as if he could have crawled into it. 'I know exactly how you feel,' he sympathized. 'I just can't do a danged thing about it.'

'So I get to ride back to the ranch and tell 'em we got no law in Wyoming Territory.'

'Poor excuse of law, at best,' Thurman agreed. 'You're plumb right. It's a raw deal, and I can't defend it. I just can't help it.'

Tad's face graphically portrayed his frustration and helpless anger.

Thurman was obviously just as unhappy about the situation. He was also tired of talking about something he could do nothing about. He deliberately changed the subject. 'You'll be ridin' out right away?'

'Pretty soon. I gotta go over to the brand office, if you can steer me thataway.'

Thurman's eyebrows rose. 'Gonna register a brand?'

'No, I need to find out who owns one. We started seein' a brand nobody knows who belongs to on calves.'

'That ain't too unusual.'

'It is when the cows are wearin' several different brands, and the calves is all still suckin', but they all got that other brand on 'em.'

'Somebody's long-ropin', huh?'

'Looks thataway. In a big way, and bein' real obvious about it. We just don't know who, or why he's bein' so obvious.'

'What's the brand?'

'T-Slash-S. My initials. And one guy that I'm sure works for Bligh has been showin' a paper that claims to be official, showin' it to be my brand. Problem is, I ain't never registered a brand in my life.'

'I don't know the brand. That's twice

I've heard of someone havin' a paper showin' who owns a brand. There seems to be a lot of sudden interest in that lately. Wilbur came over to see me a while back. Said somebody came in and registered a brand, then demanded a document from him stating that the brand was registered in that name. He'd never had anyone ask for that before. Thought it was real odd. Wondered if it was legal, or if the law required him to oblige.'

'It does seem odd. Was it that same brand?'

'Didn't ask. Didn't seem important. Didn't sound like nothin' against the law either, so there wasn't anything I could do about it anyway. Now that you mention it, though, maybe I'll meander over there with you and take a look-see.'

They walked together the block and a half to the office in question. It was back off the main street half a block. Tad would have looked for it a long time without directions or a guide.

'Howdy, Marshal,' the clerk greeted Thurman. 'Can I help you boys?'

'I'd like to find out who owns the T-Slash-S brand,' Tad announced.

The clerk's eyebrows lifted noticeably. He looked at Thurman. 'That's the one I went over to talk with you about a while back,' he reminded the marshal.

'That's the one?'

'That's the one.'

'Who's it registered to?'

'Somebody named Tad Strong.'

'That's me, all right,' Tad declared. 'The trouble is, I didn't register any brand.'

The clerk turned to a file cabinet, opened the wooden drawer, and rummaged in it for a short minute. He returned with a sheet of paper. 'That's what it says here,' he repeated. 'Tad Strong, T-Slash-S, left side.'

'You said the guy that registered it wanted a receipt?'

'Not just a receipt. He wanted a real official-looking signed document stating that brand was registered to that name. He even asked if there was some kind of seal I could put on it. 'Course we don't have any such thing.'

'But it wasn't this guy standin' here that registered it?' the marshal probed.

'Nope. Didn't look anything like him. Shorter guy. Younger. Red hair. Freckles. Looked almost like a kid, but he wore a tied-down six-shooter that didn't look like a kid's toy.'

Tad nodded. 'McCleary.'

'You know him?' the marshal responded.

Tad nodded. 'Sounds like one of Bligh's men I've run into a couple times.'

The marshal turned to the clerk. 'You got a piece of paper and a pencil, Wilbur?'

The clerk's eyebrows shot up quizzically, but he said only, 'Sure.'

It took the clerk only seconds to produce the requested items. The marshal shoved the paper in front of Tad and handed him the pencil. 'Here. Sign your name for me.'

'What?'

'Just write your name on that paper. Like as if you was signing something.'

Puzzled, Tad complied. The marshal turned it around toward the clerk. 'That the same signature, Wilbur?'

The clerk barely glanced at it. 'Not even close. Well, here. See for yourself.'

He turned the registry form around for them both to look at the signature. In stark contrast to the neat flowing letters of Tad's signature, the one on the document more closely resembled the awkward efforts of a child just learning to write its name.

'Now why would somebody want to register a brand in your name?' the marshal mused.

'To get me hung for long-ropin',' Tad responded.

The marshal nodded in agreement with the obvious. 'Sure does sound like an elaborate plan to set you up, all right.'

'Looks that way. Now what do I do?'

Thurman turned to the registrar.

'Can he unregister that brand?' he asked.

'Sure. Just write on the bottom, 'not a working brand', and sign your name.'

'Then can you give me something in writing to that effect?'

'Sure. Don't know why not, anyway. It might even help, if you can keep a rope off your neck long enough to get anyone to read it.'

'When I tell Bingham what's happened, I 'spect the word'll get around the country in a hurry.'

He rode out of Laramie hoping against hope he would have opportunity to do so before he ran headlong into an angry lynch party.

16

Rebecca pushed away from Tad's embrace. Her eyes reflected the panic that tied her stomach into knots. 'You sound like you're saying, 'Good bye!'' she breathed.

He looked long into her greenish-blue eyes. He sighed heavily. 'I hope not,' he offered.

It was far from enough. 'What do you mean, you 'hope not?''

'I'll get out alive if I can.'

'You're telling me that you're going to ride into Churchville all by yourself, confront Burly Bligh, arrest him if you can, or kill him if you can't arrest him, then ride out again?'

'Somethin' like that.'

'That's insane!'

'What else can I do?'

'You can try to get the army to intervene.'

'I talked with the US marshal about that. They'd have to get it authorized from Washington. It'd more than likely take a year or more to get the army to do anything.'

'You can talk the ranchers and homesteaders into teaming up together.'

'We already tried that. Half of 'em are scared. The other half want the law to do it.'

'So let the law do it!'

'What law?'

'The . . . the . . . there has to be some law. We're a United States Territory. That has to mean something.'

'That means the law is the United States marshal for the territory. And he's been told to keep his nose out of it. The law ain't gonna do a damn thing!'

'Tad! You do not need to swear at me.'

'I wasn't swearin' at you. I'm just sayin' there ain't a . . . a dadblamed thing the law is gonna do. The only thing left is to ride away and tell 'em to work it out themselves, or else go deal with it like they hired me to do.'

'They didn't hire you to take on Bligh's whole outfit single-handed.'

'Do you see a line of fellas behind me waitin' to side me and cover my back?'

'I don't care! I don't want you going in there alone. I forbid you to go in there alone!'

He laughed suddenly in spite of himself. 'Does that work with your school kids?'

'I mean it! I absolutely forbid you to do this!'

'I ain't one of your school kids. I stopped here 'cause I want you to know what I'm doin'. It wasn't to ask your permission.'

Her eyes went from angry to hurt and frightened. 'And you don't even care what I want you to do, or don't want you to do.'

'Of course I care. I love you. I got the idea you love me. But you don't control me.'

'If you really love me, you will not do this, this, this insane thing.'

His eyes reflected his own rising tide of anger. 'That's hittin' below the belt. You know it ain't got nothin' to do with whether I love you. It's just somethin' I gotta do. I gave my word I'd do my best to put a stop to the rustlin'. There ain't no other way to do it. That's just the way it is.'

'And you'll leave me to grieve you and be alone in the world just because you're too stubborn to use common sense.'

'That'd be better than you bein' hooked up with a coward, or a man that didn't keep his word, for the rest of your life.'

'I'd take that trade.'

'I wouldn't offer it.'

'So you're just going to go charging in to a certain death just to prove you're not afraid.'

'No. I ain't goin' chargin' nowhere, and I ain't tryin' to prove nothin'. Just doin' my job. I'll slip into Churchville quiet like. I'll try to get Bligh alone, arrest him, hog-tie him, or cold-cock him, whatever I have to, and get him out of there. Then we'll have a hearin' for him and hang 'im legal like. Without a leader, that mob at Churchville will start killin' each other soon enough, and we'll be shut of the whole bunch of 'em.'

'It doesn't have a chance. You don't have a chance.'

'Well, I guess it's kinda like faro. It ain't the best game for a fella to play. The odds are always against you. But it's usually the only game in town.'

'But nobody's forcing you to play it.'

'I guess they are. I gotta play the hand I been dealt.'

She came into his arms then, afire with passion, alive with the promise of every feminine delight that has launched armies and altered histories through all the ages of mankind. He didn't know if it was the fires of desperation, a last-ditch effort to change his mind with everything she could offer if he would just stay, or just her love for him that shattered all her restraint. Her kiss and the feel of her body pressed against him, her hands moving across his back, sent fire through every part of his being.

If she had known how close he was to breaking, she wouldn't have hesitated. She did hesitate though, for just a moment. She broke the embrace and stepped back half a step. She looked deeply into his eyes, as if trying to gauge the tenor of his resolve. It was that momentary break that allowed him to steel himself against the rising tide of his desire. As she moved to come back into his arms, he backed away, turning slightly away from her.

'I gotta go,' he hurried.

'Tad!'

'I love you, Becky Folsom,' he said over his shoulder as he hurried out the door.

The dam she had erected against her emotions ruptured. A flood of tears erupted, drowning out any ability to make a response. Her tear-bedimmed eyes could only watch in silence as he stepped into the saddle and rode away.

He was too far out of town to see her run from the house to the shed behind, hurriedly saddle her own horse, and ride out of town at a gallop.

17

The first streaks of dawn colored the eastern horizon. The day promised to be hot again, but it was cool so far. Cool enough the long coat Tad wore didn't seem terribly out of place.

It was far less jarring than his appearance without it would have been. The coat covered the fact that he was a walking arsenal.

His usual Russian .44, with all nine spots in the cylinder filled now, was in its usual place at his hip. Turned backward on the other side he wore two pistols, one directly behind the other. Both were Colt .44s.

Suspended on a cord that crossed his shoulder, a twelve-gauge Colt revolving shotgun hung against his right thigh. Six shells of double-aught buckshot filled its chambers.

Suspended from the other shoulder

so that it hung along his left thigh, his .44/.40 carbine dangled, also fully loaded. Every pocket bulged with extra shells. He was as ready as he could get.

He had waited a full day, watching the town from a high vantage point with a telescope. He already had a good idea of the lay of the town. Now he also had a sense of the habits of its denizens and the hours of his best opportunity. He could only guess that what he had observed would be somewhat of a pattern.

He had devised, while he watched and waited, a desperate plan that might, just might, allow him to either kill or capture Burly Bligh and get out alive.

It was a slim chance at best. 'Just about like a snowball's chance in hell,' he told himself realistically.

He had four horses secured in different locations outside of town. When he made a run for it, whatever direction he had to run he would at least have a mount waiting. He had all the weapons and ammunition he could reasonably carry and still function. It was the best he could do.

A picture of Becky floated in his vision for the umpteenth time since his troubled good-bye of two days ago. He knew with certainty he would never again feel the thrill of her in his arms, the taste of her lips, the surprise of her tongue darting past his own lips, the fire of her passion. A deep sense of loss threatened to sweep him away. He shook his head, forcing the images from his mind. He steeled himself against the intense sense of loss, as if he could stop feeling it by sheer force of will.

He watched from a pre-chosen vantage point as Clyde Westler made his way from his house two blocks away to the town marshal's office. He was within minutes of the same time Tad had observed yesterday. So far, the day's activities appeared to form a routine.

When Westler stepped into his office and reached for the coffee pot, Tad was silently right behind him. He jabbed the barrel of his .44 in the lawman's back. 'Don't make any quick moves, Westler,' he warned.

'What's goin' on?' Westler asked, keeping his hand well away from his own weapon.

With his off hand, Tad slid that weapon out of the marshal's holster. 'Judgment day,' he said.

'Huh?'

'Bligh's judgment day. Not yours. Not if you behave yourself.'

'Strong!' Westler breathed, glancing over his shoulder. 'You're dead. The boys seen you die.'

'Well, that relieves a lot of strain,' Tad gritted. 'If I'm already dead, I got nothin' to fear an' nothin' to lose, huh?'

'McCleary said he seen you die jumpin' off Hansen's Cliff.'

Rather than argue the point, Tad jabbed him again in the spine with his gunbarrel. 'Head for that cell. I'm gonna lock you in.'

The marshal visibly thought of several other options before moving toward the open door of the only cell in the small building. As they passed the desk, Tad swept up the key on its large ring. As the marshal walked into the cell, he started to turn. Just as he did the barrel of Tad's .44 collided smartly with the side of his head. The marshal crumpled to the floor.

Moving swiftly, Tad stuffed a rag into the marshal's mouth, securing it with his neckerchief. Then he pulled a length of rope from one of the pockets of his long coat. He tied Westler securely, his bound hands secured behind him, tied to his bound feet, giving him no way to wiggle loose or call for help. Tad locked the cell door and shoved the key into his pocket.

Looking both ways up and down the street, he crossed quickly. He made his way to the back door of The Pleasure Emporium. Looking both ways again, he slipped inside and flattened himself against the wall. His eyes adjusted quickly to the interior gloom. Nothing stirred.

The main room of the saloon was neat and orderly. The softness of the early morning light made it look less harsh and gaudy than normal. The chairs were all upended on top of the tables. Clean sawdust covered the floor. The smell of fresh sawdust nearly countered the smell of stale beer, sweat and smoke that marked all saloons. The bar was bare and polished. Glasses and mugs were inverted on flour sack dishtowels along the backbar.

Tad wished he could have figured a way inside the establishment while it was open and operating. That would have given him a much better idea of the layout of rooms that surrounded the main body of the saloon. Most of them, he knew, would be the rooms of the 'working girls' that Bligh kept for the amusement of his small army. In all likelihood, one or more of those gunmen would be in each of the rooms as well, expending their ill-gotten gain from rustling and robberies. If he chose a wrong room, he would ignite a maelstrom of gunfire he could not hope to survive. His one chance was to guess the door to Bligh's quarters accurately, to catch him still asleep, and to capture him without gunfire that would alert his henchmen. 'Now I know just how that snowball in hell feels,' he told himself silently.

At the end of the long bar, separated from the extensive row of doors, another door, somewhat larger than the rest, looked as if it were made of solider stuff than the others. It seemed the best bet before him. He shoved away from the wall and began to silently walk toward it, his steps muffled by the fresh sawdust.

He was four steps from the wall when he discovered he had guessed correctly. The door swung open and Bertram Bligh started to emerge. He stopped dead in his tracks when he spied Tad. His eyes widened. The moment of stunned surprise passed in an instant. With amazing speed his massive hand swept upward, clutching the Colt .45, his thumb cocking the hammer even as it cleared leather.

Tad was only the barest instant faster. It mattered little. The instant allowed the blast from his .44 to slam into the saloon owner, staggering him backward, causing his own shot to go wide. The second shot from Tad's pistol in almost the same instant drove him farther backward. He was dead before he spread-eagled on the deep pile of the plush burgundy carpet of his living room.

Pandemonium erupted instantly behind Tad. Doors whipped open. Scantily clad or half-dressed men exploded into the barroom from almost every door along its length. Every one held at least one gun. Every hand was skilled and deadly in its use.

Tad's .44 disappeared into its holster quicker than the eye could follow its path. In its place the Colt revolving shotgun swung up, leveled, and began roaring a message of instant death and defiance.

Holding the Colt at waist level, Tad blasted away, driving hapless victims of the mortal loads of buckshot backward into the others, as fast as he could manipulate the trigger.

Firing over their shoulders, survivors of that first deadly volley dived back into the cover of the rooms. As Tad fired in desperate haste, he walked backward, seeking the temporary shelter of Bligh's quarters. When the Colt's firing pin dropped with a click on an empty cylinder, he whirled and ducked inside the large sitting room. A solid roar of answering fire in the confined quarters sounded like the thunder of death. Wood slivers flew from the door and its frame. Ducking behind it, Tad slammed it shut, shot the heavy steel bolt home, then whirled, his .44 automatically in his hand, to see what waited for him within.

Bligh's dead body stretched on the floor at his feet. The door to his bedroom stood open. Inside the bedroom, a young woman sat bolt upright, clutching a blanket in front of her naked body. To one side of her, a dozen feet away, a window stood open to the cool air of early morning.

'Better bail out,' Tad ordered, motioning toward the window.

Without waiting for any further opportunity or taking time to search for her clothing, the woman bolted from the bed, slipped through the window, and ran.

Before she was even out of sight, bullets began slamming through that window, and every other window of Bligh's quarters. Tad could hear bullets hitting the door that opened into the barroom as well, but the door was thick and solid.

The windows were a different matter. They were all equipped with shutters built to withstand almost any common weapon, but he had no way to close them without exposing himself to the deadly hail of gunfire that probed relentlessly for him.

Hugging the floor, he crawled to one

of the windows. Keeping himself as hidden as possible, he peered from a bottom corner. He could see half a dozen men firing from behind whatever cover the street afforded. When one of them rose to his feet and sprinted to a different cover, Tad fired. He was rewarded with the unmistakable *thwack* of a leaden slug finding flesh, but he didn't watch to see its effect. He dropped instantly to the floor and scurried across to a different window. Following the same tactic, he almost immediately spotted a target and reduced the force ranged against him by one more.

He lay flat on the floor and reloaded the Colt revolving shotgun from the loads in one coat pocket. He shucked off the coat, then both of the weapons that were slung from his shoulders. He laid the Colt in the middle of the room, where he could reach it quickly from any location.

He selected another window, watched beneath the steady barrage of lead for another exposed target. When opportunity afforded, he fired, and was rewarded by a fierce curse that cut off abruptly.

He began an irregular pattern of checking windows, firing as swiftly as possible from first one, then another, keeping them guessing too much about his location to risk rushing him.

He glanced upward just as he was about to leave one of the windows, his eyes drawn to sudden movement. He spotted a gunman, with a rifle, in a tree about fifty yards from the building. His greater height would sooner or later expose Tad's position on the floor, and allow him to put an end to this madman who had dared to invade their security.

Tad stretched across the floor, shouldered his rifle, aimed and fired. The gunman toppled from the tree.

Tad retreated to the wall, propping himself against it. He was suddenly overwhelmed with the constant barrage of bullets, splintering wood, shattering objects, pounding a relentless cacophony of his certain and impending doom. He realized with a rush the enormous stupidity of thinking he could slip into Bligh's stronghold, take him out, and escape.

Now he had only to wait until the attackers, who had him hopelessly surrounded and pinned down, managed to work their way to a point against the sides of the building. Then one or more would catch an instant of opportunity when he wasn't watching that particular window, and he would die in a hail of bullets.

At least he would die thinking of Becky, and the feel of her lips against his. There was no further sense in even trying to prolong it. There were too many. Bligh was dead, but in everything else he had failed. The end was utterly inevitable. He sighed in resignation, leaned his head back against the wall, and simply waited for the bullet that would end it.

18

Bullets slammed steadily into every wall. Wood fragmented in an endless shower of splinters. Pieces of broken vases, mirrors and pictures shattered into smaller fragments. Dust rose in a thickening haze.

The impossible noise level faded to a distant roar in Tad's mind. Scenes from different times in his life passed before him, as if in a dream. Then Becky's face was there again, crowding out everything else. He studied the line of her jaw, the shape of her lips, the sparkle in her eyes. She turned and walked away from him, glancing at him over her shoulder. He studied the shape of her body, the swing of her slightly too wide hips as she walked. Then she was back in front of him again, facing him.

It puzzled him for just a moment, wondering how she could be back there so quickly when he hadn't even seen her turn around. Then he remembered it was all in his mind.

She wasn't really there. It was only the intensity of his love and longing that was there. That and the despair of his hopelessness.

He had never felt the loneliness of his life until that first day he rode into Caldwell City. He had seen something in her eyes, something in the curls of the strawberry blond hair, something in the way she carried herself, that reached out and drew him in as helplessly as a fish on a hook.

Her piercing, dry sense of humor captivated him. Her intelligence fascinated him. Her smile radiated through parts of his being he hadn't known existed.

From that moment, whenever he was in her presence he felt whole, complete, content. Whenever he left her presence, he felt suddenly empty and alone. Then he found himself counting the days, searching for excuses to return to town, just so he could talk to her, watch her walk, see her smile, feel her lips again.

He watched her face now, in the haze of his despair. He studied it, knowing it was the vision he would take to his grave, that it was the only way he would ever see her again. He counted the freckles that bridged her nose and highlighted her cheeks. He wanted her to smile, but couldn't think of how to make her do that. His forehead furrowed with the intensity of willing her smile to enlighten his life just one more time. She had to do it quickly. He only had minutes, maybe only a few seconds, before the inevitable ripping of a dozen bullets into his body.

A sudden increase in the number of shots stirred some leaden corner of his mind. They seemed, suddenly, to have a different tone. The change slowly registered through the fog of resignation and despair that had descended on Tad's mind. The image of Becky faded away. Slowly his eyes became alert again. 'Now what?' he asked aloud of no one.

Almost at once the steady fusillade of lead ripping into his rapidly disintegrating shelter diminished, then stopped altogether. The amount of shots being fired increased, but now their tone was completely different. It was suddenly directed elsewhere.

Men began cursing in steady streams of vitriol, at the top of their voices. Every curse was accompanied by another shot, but suddenly none of them were aimed at Tad.

He crept to one of the windows. Ranged in an arc behind the back of The Pleasure Emporium, gunmen were lying prone behind rocks and trees. They directed a steady stream of rifle fire into the gunmen attacking Tad's safehold, rather than at him.

Steadily, those who were able retreated around the end of the building, and from between it and the next building on the other side. Those who survived the effort took shelter in the street, lying prone amid the dust and road apples.

Realizing he had been snatched from certain death by rescuers he didn't even know, Tad stood. He took a deep breath, feeling the heavy mantle of despair slide off from his shoulders. He walked to the door leading into the barroom and slid back the heavy bolt. He swung it open.

Standing six feet from the door, waiting for him, Rusty McCleary stood motionless. An instant of shocked disbelief passed as quickly as it had risen in Tad.

'It's over, McCleary,' he said. 'Shuck off your gunbelt.'

'It ain't over yet,' McCleary responded. He grinned then, but it was a mirthless smile. It reminded Tad far more of a wolf's baring of its teeth as it prepared to kill.

'It's over,' Tad disagreed. 'There's no way you can walk away from this one.'

'I don't aim to,' McCleary responded. 'I just aim to make sure you don't either. If I ain't gonna get 'er, you ain't either.'

'That's what this has always been about with you, isn't it?'

'You know it is. She was my girl afore you showed up.'

Tad shook his head. 'She never was, and never would be. You just weren't smart enough to see she didn't want anything to do with you.'

'That's a lie!' McClearly snarled. 'Not that it matters. You ain't gonna have her neither.'

'You aren't anywhere near good enough to take me,' Tad declared. 'Just drop your gunbelt.'

'Not a chance,' McCleary shot back instantly. 'Even if you kill me instead of them guys out there, you're still a dead man.'

'Why's that?'

'They'll hang you. Your brand's on more'n thirty calves still suckin' cows with other brands on 'em. That brands you as a rustler, and the ranchers will hang you, no questions asked.'

'It won't work. The US marshal, and the ranchers, already know it was you that registered that brand in my name. The brand office in Laramie confirmed it, and notified everyone.'

Disbelief in the idea that his perfect plan had failed troubled McCleary's eyes for just a minute. Then a fierce anger took its place. With blinding speed his hand swept his Colt clear of leather.

Tad was right. McCleary wasn't nearly fast enough. The tip of his Colt's barrel was just clearing the top of his holster when a .44 slug from Tad's revolver slammed into him. His heart exploded as the heavy projectile ripped through it. His eyes looked at Tad in a split second of disbelief, then went out of focus and glazed over. He crumpled silently into the sawdust.

19

Outside of The Pleasure Emporium, new rifle fire began to stab into the numbers of Bligh's army still alive. It came from between the buildings on the other side of the street. Then two riflemen who had gained vantage points on rooftops began to systematically reduce the numbers of his attackers from above.

The beleaguered outlaws returned fire as best they could. It was clearly a losing cause. Those from behind the building were now entrenched against its sides and ranged to either direction. Bligh's followers who remained were cut off and surrounded.

Some of them broke suddenly and ran for the front door of the saloon. They were met instantly with a hail of bullets from the front windows and doors of that establishment. The unknown force that had intruded into the battle had taken over the interior of the saloon as well. There was no place left to run.

Just then a cavalry trumpet bugled the order to charge. Down the road leading into Churchville a body of soldiers approached at a gallop, three abreast. The lead man in the center held the colors of the United States Cavalry. Those at either side were already firing over the heads of their horses.

It all ended as abruptly as it had begun. Almost as though controlled by the same thought, every gunman in the street threw down his weapon as if suddenly burned by its touch. Every hand shot into the air in the universal symbol of surrender.

The cavalry unit slid to a stiff-legged stop in a cloud of dust. Troopers dropped from their horses, kneeling in firing position, holding their weapons at the ready.

From both sides of the street other

men emerged, pistols and rifles leveled at the surrendering remnants of Bligh's private army of outlaws.

One man stepped out in front of those now in command. The early rays of the morning sun reflected from the badge of a US marshal. 'You are all under arrest. Unbuckle your gun belts and let them drop. Any hidden weapons you have, drop in the dirt. If we find any still on you when you're searched, you'll die like the mangy dogs you are.'

The three outlaws hastened to comply. The marshal turned toward the sergeant who had strode forward from where his men waited. 'Good timing, sergeant. I s'pose the army'll take credit for cleanin' up this little corner of hell now.'

The sergeant grinned in response. 'Of course, Marshal.'

'Good,' Thurman surprised him by saying. 'That way I won't lose my job for insubordination.'

'Well, somebody had to ride up here,' the sergeant rejoined. 'We know you wouldn't have showed up if you didn't know the army was backin' you.'

'Why did you show up?'

'My kid told me I didn't have a choice. The company commander sorta gave his OK, but we ain't all that official neither. These men is all volunteers. I don't know how the colonel's gonna explain it to the higher-ups. Ain't my problem. I'm just a sergeant followin' orders, even if they are my kid's orders.'

'Your kid?'

'The schoolmarm in Caldwell City is my kid.'

'Is that so? What's her interest?'

'Oh, it seems somebody she's all het up about is involved here somewhere. We pertneart run our horses to death, tryin' to get here quick enough to save his hide. I don't even know if we did.'

A voice behind the pair spun them around. 'I thought you wasn't supposed to get involved up here, Marshal.'

Heck Thurman looked Tad up and down carefully. His face was bleeding from a dozen places where flying debris had broken the skin. He was covered with dust and dirt. Both sides of his shirt showed daylight through holes where bullets had missed his torso by a fraction of an inch. Only his grin seemed intact.

'I told you I had a hard time lookin' myself in the mirror to shave,' Thurman admitted. 'I knew when you left you was gonna come up here an' try to clean out this rattlesnake nest all by yourself if you had to. I just couldn't let that happen. I rounded up these boys and we rode out less'n three hours behind you.'

'You got here at a real good time,' Tad acknowledged.

'We would've been here quicker, but we didn't know you'd already opened the festivities. We stopped off at the Flying E Bar on the way. They rounded up a bunch of these other guys. You got a lot more friends than you thought you had. We had Bligh's boys pertneart outnumbered by the time we got here.

O' course, it looks to me you had the odds cut down a whole bunch all by yourself.'

Tad ignored the implied question of how he had managed to do so. 'How did Grunt know what I was doin'?'

'I guess your woman rode out and told him. He said she swapped her horse for a fresh one, and rode out again on a dead run. He was afraid she was comin' here.'

Frowning, Tad turned to the sergeant. 'How'd the army get involved?'

The grizzled old veteran looked Tad up and down even more appraisingly than the marshal. He nodded curt approval of what he saw. 'You can blame my kid. She went an' told me I oughta bring a few men up here right quick to babysit you if I ever wanted her to speak to me again.'

'Your kid?'

'I'm Becky's pa.'

Realization flooded through Tad like a shock wave. 'Well, I'll be danged. I guess I didn't never even ask her about her folks. I just figured she didn't have none, or she wouldn't be off there all by herself.'

Sergeant Folsom grinned. 'Listen, son, if she decides she's gonna go off some place and do something, the army I'm part of ain't big enough to stop her. Her ma died some years ago, but I'm still hangin' around.'

'Where is she?'

Folsom stepped to the side where he had a clearer view of the road they had so recently and hurriedly traveled. He shielded his eyes with his hand. 'She had to swap horses again, so that slowed her down some. She dang neart rode three of 'em to death. If I ain't mistook, though, that cloud o' dust back there is about due to be her.'

Tad was oblivious to the fact that he was suddenly running down the road on foot, as fast as his legs could carry him. He had run almost to the horse he had stationed in that direction before he even remembered it. When he did, he leaped into the saddle. He met

Becky a quarter of a mile farther down the road. It was hard to tell whose feet hit the ground first, whose arms first wrapped around the other, whose lips ignored the dust and dirt on the other first. It really didn't matter.

THE END

We do hope that you have enjoyed reading this large print book.

Did you know that all of our titles are available for purchase?

We publish a wide range of high quality large print books including:
Romances, Mysteries, Classics
General Fiction
Non Fiction and Westerns

Special interest titles available in large print are:
The Little Oxford Dictionary
Music Book, Song Book
Hymn Book, Service Book

Also available from us courtesy of Oxford University Press:
Young Readers' Dictionary
(large print edition)
Young Readers' Thesaurus
(large print edition)

For further information or a free brochure, please contact us at:
Ulverscroft Large Print Books Ltd.,
The Green, Bradgate Road, Anstey,
Leicester, LE7 7FU, England.
Tel: (00 44) **0116 236 4325**
Fax: (00 44) **0116 234 0205**

ARIZONA PAY-OFF

Duke Patterson

When Tex Scarron, six feet of whipcord and steel, rides home to the Bar X in Arizona, he finds Parson Dean and his gang working a lucrative 'protection' racket. Ranchers who fail to pay up find that their cattle are rustled, their homesteads are burnt down and their cowhands are shot in the back. As Tex sets out to rid the territory of the Parson, his experience of fighting hoodlums comes in handy when the gunplay gets fast and furious.

GUN LAW

Lee Walker

Aged fourteen, Jake Chalmers witnessed his parents' murder by drunken cowboys. Now he's a young man — with a gun for protection . . . On the run after killing, in self-defence, Jake arrives in Sweetwater. But he's unable to maintain a low profile when he becomes embroiled in a feud between the businessman Jordan Carter, and sheriff Luke Gardner. Then one of Carter's men murders Luke, and Jake must choose between the law of the land and the law of the gun . . .

SIX FOR LARAMIE

Rick Dalmas

Six gun-fighters come to Laramie — all hungry for money. Yet greed is not everyone's sole motive. Bannerman, the toughest and fastest, has a special reason: one of the other five has shot his friend in the back. There's no charge for what he intends to do to him, even though he knows this might disrupt the plans for the work he's been hired to do — and that it could put him on the wrong end of *five* guns!

GUN FURY

Walt Keene

When veteran gunfighter Tom Dix and his pal Dan Shaw get a telegraph message from the remote town of Gun Fury, it's from their friend Wild Bill Hickok. Realising that something perilous is brewing they saddle up and ride. Death awaits them when they reach Gun Fury — bodies soon start to pile up. Curiously, the infamous Hickok claims he never sent for them. But Dix and Shaw are trapped in Gun Fury — and fighting for their lives . . .